I0589760

CYNTHIA HICKEY

Caper's Dark Adventure

A Tiny House Mystery, Book Four
By Cynthia Hickey

ISBN: 978-1-0878-7364-0

This book is dedicated to all those who love a cozy
mystery full of fun and adventure.

Chapter One

Mr. Robinson's camper looked vacant.
Strange since the sun had been up for at least two hours.

I, CJ Turley, nosy caretaker of the tiny house community, Heavenly Acres, couldn't resist turning the doorknob in front of me. You'd think I'd have learned from my past adventures, but no…here I went again.

"Hello? Mr. Robinson?" I stepped inside. The shades were drawn—I wondered why. I didn't know the man well, but he kept the outside area clean. The exact opposite now greeted me.

An overturned ottoman, an overwhelming amount of dishes in the sink, and an overflowing trashcan made me wonder whether Mr. Robinson had been robbed…or worse.

I glanced back outside. Not seeing his golf cart anywhere, I headed to the back of the one-room home. Blankets were strewn off the bed. I couldn't tell whether a crime had occurred, or the man was simply a slob. Still, it warranted a call to my boyfriend and park ranger, Eric Drake.

"Good morning, gorgeous." Eric's smile came through the phone in his voice.

"Good morning. Have you seen Mr. Robinson today?"

"No, why?"

"His camper looks trashed and the golf cart is gone. I don't remember seeing him yesterday, either."

"Despite how clean he keeps the campsites, the interior of his home is vastly different. I'll be there in a few minutes and take a look around."

"Thank you." I hung up and stepped outside to take a seat at the concrete picnic table. Eric never failed to come to my rescue, unless he was too far away. Having someone to rely on was the best feeling ever.

While I waited, my uncle Larry Acres, and my best friend, Mags, stopped by on their daily morning walk. Before she met my uncle, Mags had been my ever-present sidekick. I had to admit I missed her. "Hey, you two."

"What's up?" Mags sat next to me. "It isn't like you to be idle on someone else's property."

"I'm waiting for Eric. Neither of us have seen Mr. Robinson in a day or two."

"That isn't unusual. The man often goes camping in the woods. You know that." She leaned back against the table and motioned for Larry to join us.

He planted a kiss on my cheek and sat next to

Mags. "You look worried."

"I've got a feeling," I said.

"Oh, no." Mags sighed. "That's never a good sign. Can't you go more than three months without finding danger?"

My eyes widened. "Who said anything about danger?" The feeling in my gut, that's who.

"I see it in your eyes." Mags gave a definitive nod. "Yep, trouble is coming. Where's that trouble-finding dog of yours?"

Caper had a talent for scouting out mysteries that may or may not—all right, always—put me in dangerous positions, but I took offense at anyone else mentioning it. "I left her at home because it looks like rain."

"Ah. What did she do now?" Mags grinned.

I sighed. "Chewed up my new phone case." I held up what had once been pink and sparkly but now was sparkless and had a jagged edge where the glitter and liquid had dripped out.

"That's unfortunate. Best get a new case before you drop your phone." Mags patted my arm, a consoling expression on her face. "Why don't you and Eric come over for supper tonight?"

"There's no room in your house." Mags's cluttered tiny house could barely fit her, much less four adults.

"Silly, we'll eat in the new gazebo Larry built. See you at five. We're having breakfast for supper and I promise to have lots of chocolate gravy." She headed for the road, pausing long enough to wave her fingers goodbye before linking her hand with Larry's and strolling away.

A light drizzle had started before Eric arrived. He jumped from his side-by-side and jogged to where I sat under an awning. "It's going to downpour in a bit." He grabbed my hand, and we dashed to the camper.

Eric stopped inside. "This is how his place always looks."

"Isn't it strange that no one has seen him, and he didn't tell anyone he was leaving?"

"A little." He glanced around the room. "What's even stranger though is that the gun cabinet is unlocked and his rifle is gone. Hunting season doesn't start for another week."

I hadn't recognized that the curio cabinet holding deer figurines was also a gun cabinet. "Maybe he's poaching?"

Eric shook his head. "He wouldn't do that. Do you have a raincoat in your cart?"

"Yes, why?"

"We're going for a ride." He gave me a lopsided smile and dashed back to his side-by-side.

I fetched my clear raincoat from my cart, put it on and pulled up the hood, then hurried to join him. "Should we stop and get Caper?"

Eric laughed. "If something's amiss, she'll find out what. Sure, let's go get her."

Twenty minutes later the rain fell in buckets and a happy pup sat on the seat between us. I ruffled the hair between her ears. "You're a handful, you know that?" I'd fallen in love with the rowdy puppy I'd inherited when my grandmother died. I glanced at Eric. "Any idea where we're going?"

"His favorite camping place when he wants to be

alone. It'll take about an hour. There's snacks and water bottles in the back." He reached over and squeezed my hand. "Don't worry. We'll find him sitting happily by a campfire with a cup of coffee in his hand. Don't borrow trouble."

"It's like you don't even know me." I grinned.

"Oh, but I do." He leaned over and gave me a quick kiss. "Why are you looking for Robinson anyway?"

"I received an email that I think is meant for him." I pulled a sheet of paper from my pocket. "Someone wants to reserve spot ten. We no longer have a number ten, so it has to be for Blue Lake Campground." After the last three mysteries I was involved in included, to some extent, house number ten, I'd asked the landowner to remove the tiny house and make the plot a community garden. He'd agreed, and I couldn't wait until spring to plant some vegetables.

"I suppose it could mean site 110, and someone forgot to add the one." Eric shrugged. "Not many people camp this time of year. The mornings and nights are too cold."

That's what I'd thought upon receiving the email, but the world held a surprising number of weird people. Plus, some people still camped in campers rather than tents, so I hadn't thought too much about it.

I leaned back and propped my feet on the dashboard, listening to the rain hit the canvas roof over us. In the warmer weather, the canvas stayed folded in the back, but today I was grateful for its covering. I shivered under my sweatshirt and raincoat, wishing I'd worn my boots.

"Would you rather we turn around?" Eric cast me a quick glance.

"No, I'll warm up eventually."

"There's a blanket in that bag in the back."

"Awesome." I knelt and leaned over the seat.

The vehicle hit a pothole. My head banged the pole holding up the canvas. I somersaulted over the seat and landed on my back in the mud. I hated mud. Mud brought on a fear of drowning after I'd almost died face down in the mud almost a year ago. I stared at the sky and blinked against the rain. I might drown, but it would be by rain this time.

Eric leaned over me. "Can you move? I'm so sorry. I didn't realize the hole was quite that deep."

I wiggled my feet, then held up a hand. "I'll take that blanket now."

He frowned. "Did you hit your head? Does anything hurt?"

"No, I mean, yes. I hit my head on the pole, but now that the breath has returned to my lungs, nothing hurts."

He pulled me to my feet and into his arms. "I really am sorry."

"Maybe I should drive." I smiled up into his face.

"Sweetheart, we'd both wind up in the mud then." He cupped my face and kissed me before helping me back in the vehicle, then fetched the blanket and wrapped it around me. "Let's go find our friend."

The rain continued to pour from a slate-gray sky until the cold wet seeped into my bones. I really hoped Mr. Robinson had a fire going so I could dry off.

"Almost there." Eric drove across a shallow creek and up a hill.

The further we went, the more convinced I was that our friend had started hunting early. Unless he hunted on private land with permission, Eric would have to issue him a fine. It wouldn't be easy for my kindhearted man.

"Here we go."

Through the trees I spotted a bright yellow tent. "Thank goodness."

We parked next to the tent and a sodden fire pit. I glanced around, disappointed not to see a fire. "Do you think he's in the tent?"

"Maybe. Go on, Caper, do your thing." Eric set my dog on the ground.

She shook her fur against the rain, then darted toward the tent. Caper wasn't a dummy. She knew tents often held food.

I jumped down and followed her inside. The last thing Mr. Robinson would want is torn bags of food strewn around. I parted the flap. "Caper?"

My eyes adjusted to the gloom.

Sure enough, Mr. Robinson held a coffee cup in his hand. What marred the picture before me was the bullet hole in the center of his forehead.

Chapter Two

Tears spilled from my eyes, and I sagged against the tent wall. Since it was made from material, I stumbled backward through the opening and found myself once again on my back staring toward the sky. "He's inside," I said.

Eric must have known something was wrong from the look on my face because he ducked into the tent like a shot had been fired. "Call Davis, CJ."

I struggled up and hurried back to the vehicle, still crying. I might have called him Mr. Robinson, but he was a friend. Someone who'd helped me during my early days as overseer of the tiny house community. I grabbed my phone from the seat which had thankfully slipped from my pocket earlier and dialed Davis, our small town's detective.

"Mr. Robinson is dead," I said.

"Excuse me?"

"Someone shot Mr. Robinson." I sniffed.

9

"Where are you?"

"I have no idea, but you need to come." I swiped my hand across my eyes. "It's where he likes to camp."

"I know the place. It will take me awhile. Is Eric with you?"

I nodded, then realized he couldn't see me. "Yes."

"Don't touch anything." Click.

Caper leaned on my leg and stared up at me with soulful brown eyes. "You did it again," I said. "Why are you always finding dead people or…things?"

She barked and wagged her tail.

I patted her head. Grandma had aptly named the pup when she'd called her Caper. Not wanting to see Mr. Robinson again, I yelled to Eric that Davis was on his way, then grabbed a water bottle and guzzled half in one go.

"Are you alright?" Eric stared into my face.

I shook my head. "Not really. Who would want to kill him? Everyone liked him." I leaned into his chest.

"It's obvious someone didn't. Help me search the tent for clues without touching anything." He pulled gloves from his pocket. "I've covered up the body."

He actually wanted my help? Wow. Usually, people told me to let matters be. I pulled on the gloves and followed Eric into the tent. After a quick glance at a sleeping bag covering Mr. Robinson, I started digging through grocery bags of food items. Finding nothing there, I turned to the ice chest and opened the lid.

Inside, wrapped in freezer paper and gallon-size

storage bags were assorted packages of venison. "He's been poaching."

Eric peered into the cooler, then removed one of the packages. "I don't believe it."

"It's right in front of us." I shoved my hand into the cooler of half-melted ice and retrieved a baggie that held an assortment of photographs. "Look at this."

Eric took the baggies and spread them across a small cooking table. Several men stood next to two deer. Unfortunately, the men were turned so we couldn't see their faces. "These are the poachers."

"One of them might be our friend. Look. That man is wearing the same red cap."

Eric shook his head. "This is what Davis will think, too. I'm going to prove my friend's innocence. I refuse to believe he would shoot deer out of season." Another picture revealed the buck heads minus the bodies. Still another showed the bodies cast aside as garbage. "Trophy hunters."

Could Mr. Robinson have come across the discarded carcasses and skinned them so as not to waste the meat? Had the poachers discovered him and killed him to keep him quiet? With every passing second, more questions arose.

"I'll help you figure out what happened."

"No, this is my job. You can help by watching over the campground until a replacement can be found." The tone of his voice left no room for argument. I'd hear the same thing again from Davis. Mr. Robinson had been my friend, too. I'd do some investigating of my own with the help of my friends.

"I can read your face." Eric frowned. "Absolutely

not. Every time you get involved, someone tries to kill you."

"And each time I get a little bit smarter and more skilled." I crossed my arms and left the tent. *Thank you, God, for stopping the rain.* Unfortunately, the wood near the fire pit was too wet to light. I retrieved the blanket from the side-by-side and climbed onto the seat to wait for Davis. I woke to Eric turning the key in the ignition. "Has Davis come?"

"Come and gone. The coroner is removing the body now and the place is an active crime scene. Time for us to go."

"Would you send the photos to my email, please?"

"What makes you think I took photos of the pictures?" He raised a brow.

"Because I know my man." I grinned and closed my eyes. If he didn't send them to me, I'd do it myself when he left his phone lying around.

He groaned, most likely reading my mind again. "Fine. I'll do it as soon as we get home."

"I can do it now while you drive," I offered, still smiling.

"You're incorrigible." He handed me his phone and headed home.

As he drove, I emailed myself the pictures, then mourned some more the loss of my friend. "Do you think I should let the owner of Heavenly Acres know about Mr. Robinson or wait and let the authorities tell him or her?" I had yet to meet my boss since everything was done via internet.

"Let Davis handle it. Why?"

"I'd really like to take on the campground in

addition to my regular duties. With the help of Roy Olson and his wife, plus a routine I stick to on a daily basis, I find myself with a lot of extra time and could use something to fill it. Not to mention working the campground would allow me to question the campers who braved the cold and arrived for deer season."

"I know you have an ulterior motive, but I'll found out who to contact." He put his hand on my leg. "Be careful snooping, CJ. I'll be busy trying to help Davis find these men."

"I will. I promise." Hopefully, those wouldn't be famous last words.

By the time we arrived home, night had fallen, and I curled up on the sofa in my house and cuddled my dog. Eric had opted to go home to change and discuss the next day's plans with Davis. I shed some more tears for Mr. Robinson, then clipped Caper's leash on her collar and headed to Mags's.

When I knocked on her door, she took one look at my face and ushered me inside. "What happened?"

I plopped onto her floral, doily-covered sofa. "Someone shot Mr. Robinson."

"No!" She covered her mouth, dropping beside me. "I once wanted to date that man."

I frowned. What a thing to say at a time like this. "We found him in his favorite campsite in the woods. Either he was poaching deer or ran across people who were." I explained about the photos and deer meat.

"Let me see the photos. I'm so excited to have another case to work on."

My scowl deepened. "Aren't you upset about our friend's death at all?"

"Of course, I am, but we can't bring him back. So let's see that justice is done." A manic gleam shone in her eyes.

"You're a monster." I handed her my phone.

"Oh, pooh. You're as addicted to mysteries as I am. I never had this much fun before you took this job. Things were rather boring before." She flipped through my phone. "Larry's a hunter. Maybe he would recognize these guys."

It was a long shot. "I'll show them to him tomorrow. Sorry we missed supper tonight."

"We postponed until tomorrow when you weren't here by late afternoon." She sprang up and bustled to her small galley kitchen. "You need tea."

I didn't want tea. I wanted my bed, but I also didn't want to hurt anyone's feelings and bringing me tea would make Mags feel better about the murder of our friend. I narrowed my eyes in her direction. *If* she felt bad.

She did. My tears started again at the sight of hers trickling down her cheeks.

I set Caper on the floor and rushed to Mags's side and pulled her into a hug. "We'll find out who did this."

"I know we will. We haven't failed yet." She patted my back and stepped away. "Tonight, we mourn, tomorrow we plan." She dropped a chamomile tea bag into a cup and poured hot water over the top. "Do you want something stronger added?"

I shuddered. "No thank you." While I didn't mind if others imbibed, I tended to stay away from alcohol other than the occasional glass of wine. I watched while Mags added peppermint-flavored vodka to her cup, then she led me back to the sofa.

"Larry won't let me help you if he isn't involved." She lifted her cup and peered at me over the rim.

I shrugged. A few months ago, my uncle had been a suspect. Now, as a former military police, he would be invaluable.

"Are you going to call Ann?"

Again, I shrugged. Ann Lowery, police officer, now private investigator, had been assigned to keep me safe many times, poor thing. We'd become great friends through it all, but she'd try to dissuade me. If things got really bad, I'd hire her, but not right now. "Probably not. The fewer involved the better."

"You're right. She'd only want to do things by the book." She chuckled. "Robinson deserves more than legal investigating."

Caught mid sip, I spewed my tea. "Let's not break the law, okay?"

"Look what you did. My doily!" She removed ten knickknacks, then shook the tea drops from the doily on the coffee table. "I'll have a hard time getting these spots out."

"Sorry." I glanced around for her evil cat. Since Caper rested under the table, the cat had to be in the loft. Good. "I'll buy you another one."

"These aren't bought, CJ. I made them. Every single one." She shook her head and went to the sink. She turned on the water and dropped the doily into it. "We'll soak it overnight. Drink up and go home. We've work to do in the morning."

I took another sip and carried my cup to the sink.

Mags was right. I needed a good night's sleep and I needed to find out who to contact in order to do Robinson's job. I'd done it before but only on a temporary basis as a favor to him. We hadn't gone through his employer.

I wasn't sure why doing his job was so important, only that by doing so, I could fill my time and find his killer. Smart? Most likely stupid, but anyone who knew me knew that once I got involved, there was no turning.

Grabbing the end of Caper's leash, I told Mags I'd see her in the morning and headed to the front door to the sound of hissing. A stinging in my ankle told me the cat had found me and somehow managed to get her claws up the leg of my pants.

"Bad kitty." I shook her off and rushed outside, slamming the door behind me. "Seriously, Caper, you need to put that cat in her place."

I made it halfway across the street, then froze. An unfamiliar truck, complete with an eight-pound rack attached to its hood, idled in front of my house. Not sure whether to see who they were or to flee, I opted for flight and raced back inside Mags's house.

Chapter Three

The next morning, I cleaned the cat scratches on my ankle, then hobbled down the stairs to make coffee. The strange truck didn't leave until almost midnight. I called Davis, then Eric, but neither answered their phones.

While the coffee dripped into my cup, I peeked through the kitchen window curtains. No sign of the truck or anyone else for that matter. A quick glance at the thermometer showed a chilly thirty-nine degrees. Brr. Only an idiot would be outside for any length of time.

My phone rang. The screen showed it to be Eric. With cup in hand, I settled on the sofa and answered, "Good morning."

"Good morning." His deep voice never failed to send my heart into somersaults. "Sorry I couldn't answer the phone last night. Davis and I were on stakeout."

"My guess is you didn't see anyone."

"Good guess."

"Not a guess." I blew into my cup. "I called because a strange truck with antlers sat outside my house last night."

"What?"

I repeated what I'd said. "I stayed at Mags's until almost midnight when it finally drove off. Do you think it's the people you're looking for?"

"Most likely. Why else would they be there? Stay put. I'll contact Davis and be right over." He hung up.

I propped my feet on the coffee table fully intending to follow orders, at least until the sun warmed up the day. Riding around in a golf cart in cold weather was not something I called enjoyable.

Caper scratched at the door to go out. With a sigh, I set my cup down and stepped into the cold to attach her to the line I'd tethered outside to prevent her from wandering off. By the time I got back in the house, my feet felt frozen. I closed the door, locked it, then retrieved my cup, and stood at the window to wait until Caper did her business.

My hand holding the cup froze midair. The same truck I'd seen the night before cruised past my house and down the road. I hurried to the bathroom window and watched it drive the circle, then leave via the front exit. I didn't have any empty houses to rent so they had to be looking for me or Eric. My hand started shaking so bad I had to set my cup down.

A key turned in the front door lock. The door swung open and Caper ran in, followed by Eric and Davis.

"Did you see it?" I hurried to greet them.

"See what?" Davis frowned.

"The truck just drove the circle and left." I crossed my arms. "If you go now, you might catch it. They turned right, toward the campground."

Davis darted out the door.

Eric plopped on the couch and held out his arms. I stepped into them and let him settle me on his lap. "You okay?"

"I am now." I nestled my head on his shoulder. "Someone must have been watching us when we found Mr. Robinson."

"Yep."

"My past must have preceded me, and they expect me to hunt them down."

"Yep."

I smiled. "You must have accepted the inevitable in knowing they're correct."

He chuckled. "Yep."

"Is that all you've got to say?" I sat up and narrowed my eyes.

"I've already called Ann. She'll be here in two days."

"Where is she?"

"On assignment in Hawaii, lucky thing."

I guess there were perks to being a PI. Especially if you had wealthy clients, which she sometimes did. "I wish you hadn't involved her."

"You haven't done a single thing yet, and already you're being watched."

"True." I climbed off his lap and sat next to him. "I do tend to attract trouble."

"Mild understatement."

"What's the plan?"

He glanced sideways. "The plan is for me and Davis to find these guys before you get too involved."

"Okay, so what's the plan?" I smiled and tilted my head.

"I see a lot of frigid mornings and evenings in my future."

"You're safe from my interference there." I hated the cold. Mags and I would formulate a plan to work on during the warmer part of the day.

I started to get up when someone knocked on the door, only to have Eric hold me back. "I'll get it." He peered through the peephole. "It's Davis." He unlocked the door and let the detective in.

"I lost them." Davis sat across from us. "Describe the truck, please."

I took a deep breath. "Dark green, jacked up on big tires, antlers on the hood, a real redneck kind of truck. I think there might have been a gun rack in the back window." I grinned, proud of myself. The experiences I'd had over the last year taught me to pay close attention to details. "Two people, although I couldn't tell if they were male or female. The license plate was too muddy to see the numbers."

Davis wrote it all down, then pierced me with a stare. "I know I've said this before, but you really should consider a career in law enforcement."

"No, thanks. I like my job."

He made a noise in his throat and climbed to his feet. "Stay out of this, CJ."

Poor man. He said it every time to no avail.

My answer was a smile. "I'll let you know if they

show up again."

When he left, Eric told me the park had agreed to let me work the campground. By summer, they'd determine whether to let me continue since they preferred an overseer who lived on the property. Since I lived across the lake, they'd go with me for now. He gave me a tender kiss, made me promise again to be careful, then left to make his rounds.

The first thing I did was pop a bagel in the toaster oven, then spread cream cheese on it. I shrugged into my coat and headed to my cute red golf cart with Caper by my side.

As was the norm, I drove the circle making mental notes of what needed doing. None of the residents were out this early except for Roy who emptied the trash bins. He waved and climbed into his cart. Cold weather left little for us to do.

I drove past the lot where number ten once stood, thankful the cursed house was gone. When springtime came, we'd be eating fresh vegetables. To make up for the house being gone, the owner had placed a new house in a new spot and given it the number twenty-six. With hunting season approaching, all rentals were full, and no full-time residents had moved out. I couldn't help but feel a lot of pleasure at a job well done.

When I'd made the circle, Mags was waiting next to my house. "I'm ready," she said.

"I've got to check the campground." I told her about being temporary overseer. "We can talk as we go."

"Great." She climbed onto the passenger seat, making Caper scoot over. "Two pairs of eyes are better than one. Maybe your deer killers are camping there."

That would be sweet but doubtful. With a truck as recognizable as theirs, I didn't figure they'd park in the open.

With the campground less than half full, the campers were scattered with plenty of room between each. The rumble of generators filled the air with the stench of fuel. At one end, a deer hung on the skinning rack, in place for the season. A man in his sixties was skinning it with precision.

I stopped the cart. "A little early for killing, isn't it?"

"Today's Saturday, lady."

Oh, right. The season had officially started for hunters using muzzle loaders. "My apologies." With a sheepish grin, I continued.

"You need to stay up on things," Mags said. "That was embarrassing. You'd think I'd be used to your actions by now."

"Did you know the season started today?"

"No, but I don't need to know. You do."

I rolled my eyes and kept driving. Not seeing anything out of the ordinary, I parked in front of Robinson's camper. "I wonder if he has family to clean out his things."

"A son, I think."

"How do you know that?" I narrowed my eyes.

"Remember? I wanted to spend time with the man, which meant I checked him out." She smirked. "I even googled him, ready to make my move, then I met Larry."

"All right then, Miss Smarty-Pants. How do we

get ahold of his son?"

She shrugged. "No idea, but the authorities will handle that type of thing. We need to go inside before they put crime-scene tape around everything."

"Good idea." I'd already been inside but hadn't done any deep searching. "Come on, Caper. You'll have to warn us if someone is coming."

Mags paused when I pushed the door open. "Was his door unlocked when you were here earlier?"

"Yes, why?" I glanced over my shoulder.

"Robinson always locked his door. Now, you've gone and messed up fingerprints. Davis is going to kill you."

Drat. Too late now. I darted back to the cart and retrieved two pairs of latex gloves. I'd learned a thing or two. "Let's disturb as little as possible."

"You don't need to tell me." She tapped her finger against her temple. "Always thinking, I am."

"Right." I fought the urge to roll my eyes and stepped inside the camper. Being only twenty-seven feet long, it wouldn't take too much time to search. I desperately wanted to clean as I went. "I'll take the bedroom and bath. You take the living area."

"Got it." I veered left while Mags went right.

This time, I treated the place as a crime scene and not just a pigsty. I lifted the blankets off the floor and shook them out before lifting the mattress to the storage area beneath. The foul odor of unwashed clothes slapped me. A strange place for a laundry basket, but whatever. I dug around a little, then let the mattress fall back into place.

Two small closets with drawers underneath stood on each side of the bed. One held a major jumble of paid bills and receipts. The other held socks and underwear. I had no time to dig through all the receipts and doubted any pertained to deer poaching anyway.

I moved to the tiny bathroom and pulled the door closed. A small cabinet next to the sink and another one below revealed nothing out of the ordinary. I hoped Mags had better luck.

"Uh, CJ?"

"Yeah?" I opened the door and stared into the wide eyes of Mags.

CJ barked like a maniac at the front door.

"That deer truck is outside, and they seem awfully interested in Robinson's storage shed."

Chapter Four

When one of the men glanced toward the camper, I put my hand on Caper's muzzle. "Shh." I reached over and slowly turned the lock on the door, then ducked out of sight, waving for Mags to do the same.

When no more sounds came from our direction, the man seemed to have changed his mind about investigating and joined his comrade at the shed. A dead bolt kept them from entering.

"Can you see their faces?" Mags peered over the windowsill.

"No. Their hats are pulled too low and those stupid hoodies keep their faces in the shadows." We weren't dealing with dummies. Nor did they seem very polite, considering the curses flowing from their lips when they couldn't get the shed open.

One of them turned in our direction. I put my hand around Caper's muzzle and held her tight. Mags scooted behind a counter.

The doorknob turned. "It's locked."

"I swear I heard a dog. Did that old man have a dog?"

"I don't know. If he did, we can't leave it here to starve. Find something to break a window."

I shot Mags a wide-eyed look. We couldn't be caught.

"Give them Caper," she mouthed.

I shook my head. No way would I sacrifice my pup.

The window over the small fold-down table shattered.

Caper yelped and jumped out of my arms, barking with enough frenzy to shake her furry little body. She jumped against the door with all four feet, turning in a somersault.

"There she is, the little beauty."

I peered around the corner as a long arm reached in and scooped up my dog. I held out my hand as if to stop him, then recoiled as Caper disappeared through the broken window. This wasn't the first time she'd been stolen since my ownership, but it was the first time I wouldn't know where to find her.

"Ow!" One of the men cried. "The little beast bit me. Look, I'm bleeding."

"Shut up and let's go."

Caper yelped.

I sprang to my feet and rushed to the window just in time to see the deer truck speed away. My shoulders slumped.

"Don't worry." Mags put a hand on my shoulder. "We'll find your dog. All we have to do is look for someone with a bite mark on their hand."

"Right." I glared. "We'll walk up to every redneck in the vicinity and ask to see their hand." I yanked the door open and stormed to the golf cart.

A nearby yip brought tears to my eyes. Caper slid from under the camper and leaped into the cart. I hugged her close. "Clever girl."

"See?" Mags arched a brow as she took her seat. "I told you we'd find her."

I rolled my eyes and headed home. My little fighter deserved a treat, and I had a phone call to Davis to make.

After giving Caper two bacon-flavored dog jerkies, I dialed Davis only to get his voice mail. I left him a message about our morning's excitement, then told Mags we were headed back to the camper.

"Why?" She frowned.

"To put up crime-scene tape in hopes of discouraging those guys if they come back."

"You have some?"

I nodded. "I took some from Ann's car when she was staying here." Of course, I could have gone to Grams's house that Ann rented from me and 'borrowed' some. But, that seemed more of a violation of privacy than from the trunk of her car which had been parked in front of my house.

"Smart thinking." Mags jumped up from the sofa and rushed out the door, calling over her shoulder for me to leave Caper behind. "Those guys will recognize her."

I didn't mention that they obviously knew who I was, considering they'd passed my house twice since Eric and I found Robinson. Instead, I dug the tape and bolt cutters out of a box in the back of the cart, set them on the seat between Mags and me, and sped back to the camper.

I tied one end of the tape to a tree, circled the camper and shed, then tied the tape to the same tree making one large circle. The tape wouldn't dissuade a hardened criminal, but it would be an extra charge against them if they were caught. When finished, I grabbed the bolt cutters and headed for the shed.

"What are you doing?" A deep voice sounded from around the camper.

I whirled and came face-to-face with Officer Milton. I'd become a major pain in his backside over the last year. "You scared me."

"You're trespassing."

"No, I'm not. I'm the temporary overseer and can't find the key to this shed. I need the supplies inside." I positioned the bolt cutters and voilà, the lock fell to the ground.

"Crime-scene tape, Miss Turley?" Milton crossed his arms.

"I put it there. Why are you here?" The door opened with a loud squawk.

"Davis called me saying he got a rambling message from you, and for me to come check it out. You weren't home, so I came here." He reached over and took the cutters from me. "What exactly are you looking for?"

"A reason someone wanted Mr. Robinson dead." I squeezed past him and reached over head to turn on the light.

What greeted me was so different from the inside of the camper. Tools hung on peg boards. A metal filing cabinet sat in one corner. Lawn equipment was neatly stacked in the corner. On a top shelf were labeled plastic bins. Obviously, Mr. Robinson cared more for organization in his job than his personal life.

The snap of latex gloves caused me to jump. I glared over my shoulder at Milton who had donned them. "You are not a nice man."

He grinned and reached to the top shelf, pulling down a bin. "Why don't you check the filing cabinet?"

"You're going to let me help?" My eyes widened.

"Sure, why not. You'll just come back later when I might not be around to protect you."

"I take it back. You have a few nice moments." The filing cabinet was locked, but a quick search inside a drawer of nails revealed the key.

Pages of information on people who had rented campsites filled the top drawer. I recognized the names of the women who had stolen diamonds and my dog once. They'd rented a site long term until their crimes caught up with them. Mr. Robinson had noted names, make of vehicles, and license plates. "It'll take a month of Sundays to go through all these." I started pulling them out and making a pile. "Is there an empty box or bin anywhere?"

Milton shoved a plastic bin with his foot toward me. "The only reason I'm allowing you to take those files is because you are temporarily in charge and this is not yet a legal crime scene."

I smirked. As if that would stop me. Had he learned nothing from knowing me? Davis and Milton kept threatening to arrest me if I didn't stop snooping but so far had failed to do so. I hoped my luck would continue.

When I'd emptied drawer number one, I moved to the next one. This contained personal papers and paid bills. After a quick flip through, I didn't find anything of interest. The third drawer held plastic sleeves of photos. I added those to the box holding files.

"Trouble coming," Mags called from outside.

I raced out. "Where?"

"There." Mags pointed at Davis's car pulling onto the grounds.

Scowling, he stopped the car and marched toward us. "Who put up the tape?"

"I did." I crossed my arms.

"Good. Saves me time. Since this is now a crime scene, you and Mags may leave."

"It's my job to be here." I paused. "Fine. Let me get my key." Before he could stop me, I unlocked and opened the back window of the shed and tossed out the things I wanted to take home. I closed and locked the window, pulled my keys from my pocket and stepped back outside, jingling them in Davis's direction. He might be dating my friend and Mags's granddaughter, Amber, but he could be a real "stick to the rules" kind of a guy.

I snarled in his direction and climbed back into my cart. I knew a back way from the lake that would get me close to where I'd tossed the bin.

"You gave in awfully easy," Mags said. "Davis will be suspicious."

"I need to retrieve the bin." I drove toward the lake and parked the cart. "Stay here. I'll be back. It'll be quieter with one." Setting off at a jog, I spotted the bin.

Thank you, God, for letting it roll a little ways downhill.

I hefted it in my arms and sneaked back to the cart. Glancing back, I caught sight of Davis watching me with a scowl on his face. Busted, but free. I curtsied and set the bin in the cart.

"Now what?" Mags glanced in Davis's direction.

"We head into town and copy all this onto a jump drive. Davis will confiscate these first chance he gets."

"I'm starting to get tired of breaking the law." Mags brushed a dry leaf off her pants. "Amber says it puts strain on her relationship with Davis."

I almost hit the brakes. "That doesn't sound like you."

She shrugged. "I know I used to be a bit harsh with my granddaughter, but now that we've reconciled, I feel as if I should do my part."

"Really?" Huh. I never would have thought it possible.

Mags chuckled. "Not really. I said it out loud to see how the idea tasted. Rather sour, if you ask me. I'm still your partner in crime."

I joined in with her laughter. "I'm glad to hear it." Although she did have a point when it came to our gumshoeing. There was a fine line between breaking the law and skirting the line. I needed to do better and not be so hardheaded. I'll admit to sometimes causing Davis's job to be harder than it needed to be.

"We need to be more subtle," I said, pulling the cart alongside my car. I popped the trunk and transferred the bin. We had maybe an hour before Davis arrived to take it away.

Thankfully, the copy store wasn't busy, and the files zipped from the copier to a jump drive in less than twenty minutes. It took another ten to copy all the paper files. I thought it might be easier to have my own in both formats.

I paid the bored young man behind the counter, pocketed the drive, and sped home. I'd no sooner set the original bin inside my front door than Davis pulled up. I smiled at my luck, hoping it would continue, and hoped he wouldn't ask to see my trunk.

"I'm here for the evidence, CJ." He stared at me with a stony expression. "Pull a stunt like that again, and I'll arrest you."

"Yeah, yeah." I'd heard that before. I retrieved the bin and handed it over. "I didn't have time to look through it."

"Good." He placed it in his backseat. "Eric said to tell you he'll bring Chinese food for supper." He got into his car and drove away.

"Well, pooh." Mags put her hands on her hips. "I thought you were eating at my place."

"It's too cold to eat outside." I put a hand on her shoulder. "You and Larry come squeeze into my house. You know Eric always brings enough."

"Okay. Don't start looking at that jump drive without me." She marched across the street to her home.

Good thing I hadn't made any promises because I inserted the jump drive into my laptop as soon as I could.

Chapter Five

My eyes were bleary by the time Eric brought supper. Right behind him came Mags and Larry. Busted again.

"You went through it." She planted her hands on her hips. "If that food Eric's carrying didn't smell so good, I'd turn around and go home."

"Sorry, but I couldn't help myself." I stood and gave Eric a kiss. "Just in time. I think my eyes are crossing." I unfolded the table from behind the sofa and set it over the coffee table while Larry grabbed the only two straight back chairs I had. Seconds later, Eric and I sat on the sofa with the other two facing us. My house might be tiny, but it had all I needed. Especially when filled with friends.

"Find out anything?" Eric handed me a small container of egg drop soup.

"I've only gotten halfway through the photos. I'm taking my time, really studying each person in them. So far, I haven't seen anyone remotely close to the two men we spotted at Mr. Robinson's camper." I sipped the soup. "I hadn't realized how many photos were taken of the community and camping get-togethers."

"If you'd waited, I could have helped." Mags narrowed her eyes.

"It's not a lot of help if we only have one laptop," I said in defense. "You'd have to download the photos because there's also only one drive."

"You're full of excuses." She bit into a wonton. "There's safety in numbers, you know."

"Fine. I'll wait until morning to look at the rest." I sighed and forked kung pao chicken into my mouth. Concentrating wasn't easy with someone commenting over her shoulder. Been there, done that. Mags would stop me, have me go back, then decide she hadn't seen anything after all.

"I take it you didn't tell Davis you made this drive." Eric arched a brow.

"Of course not." I grinned. "But he should know me by now. You won't tell, will you?"

He shook his head. "Not as long as you keep him in the loop on anything you might find. I've not found anything other than a few deer carcasses."

"You should stick around here. The culprits seem to be showing up on a regular basis." I reached for the fried rice.

"That's my problem. I'm more worried about what's happening around you then I am my job."

I put a hand on his arm. "I'm sorry, but I really want to catch whoever killed Mr. Robinson. Any word on his funeral?"

"Not yet. The ME hasn't released the body, and no one can get ahold of his son. Neighbors said they hadn't seen him in a long time, but that wasn't unusual for a traveling photographer." He dropped his plastic fork in his Styrofoam container. "Tomorrow, Davis wants to canoe up the river to see whether our suspects are roughing it in a tent."

I shuddered. After my last camping experience, I wasn't sure I'd be back in a canoe or kayak any time soon. Bad people tended to hide in the forests of the Ozarks. "Be careful."

He smiled. "That's like the car telling the tire not to turn. You are definitely not one to talk."

Laughing, I started to clean up the leftovers. "You're right, but I mean it anyway."

"Don't worry," Larry said, helping Mags to her feet. "I'll look after these two troublemakers."

"Thanks. It's good to have you around." Eric gave me a quick kiss. "I've got to go. We're leaving at dawn." He pressed his forehead against mine. "I'll be home by dark."

"Promise?"

His lips curled. "I'll do my best."

"Keep your phone on." After my last mishap, we had trackers on each other's phones.

Another kiss and he followed Mags and Larry out the door. I snapped my fingers for Caper to follow me to bed.

The next morning I woke to a loud knocking on my door and Caper's frenzied yapping. I grabbed the Taser Mags insisted I keep within reach and scurried down the stairs. A quick peek through the curtains revealed Mags with a carafe and two coffee cups.

Bless her.

"It's early, but I forgive you because you brought coffee." I snapped Caper's collar to her outdoor tether and joined Mags inside.

Seeing her already hunched over my laptop, I frowned and moved the coffee tray. "Not near my computer. If you spill, it's ruined. Set your cup on the counter, not on the table next to my laptop."

"I'm careful—oops." Mags grabbed a napkin and wiped the spot from where I had just moved my laptop. "I see what you mean."

I glared and set the laptop back. "I'm serious. Do. Not. Spill. Otherwise we lose everything." I sat next to her and booted up the laptop.

"I forgot how so not a morning person you are." She leaned close to the screen. "That's the picnic by the lake."

"Yes. I'm studying each man in every photo. They seem to be either too small or too big to be our suspects."

"We're looking for the two who are just right." She chuckled at her cleverness.

Chipper and me did not mesh in the morning. Not until I got halfway through my second cup of coffee. Caper yipped outside, signaling she wanted to come in. I gave Mags a warning look, then hurried to the door.

The engine of a truck rumbled near the gate. I glanced up to see a navy blue jeep. While it relieved me not to see the deer truck, I couldn't stop the shivers that skittered down my spine. As the jeep continued to idle there, I thought maybe the driver wanted to know if we had any vacancies.

Wrapping my arms around me to ward off the cold, I headed toward them. The jeep backed up and sped away. Great. I had to worry about every unknown vehicle that came in my vicinity. Eric and Davis would have fits.

The thing that concerned me though, more than the knowledge of being watched, was that I'd done nothing since finding Mr. Robinson's body. I hadn't even begun to snoop when the first truck made its appearance.

"What's wrong?" Mags asked the minute I entered the house and locked the door.

I told her about the jeep and my concerns. "It can't be because I've been in the newspaper a few times since helping the authorities, can it?"

"Maybe, but you aren't exactly a celebrity around here. More like…people avoid you so you won't be nosing into their private business." She wiggled her eyebrows.

"You're hilarious." I reached for my coffee. It might be time to hire Ann. I sighed and took a sip, burning my lip. So far, the day didn't promise to be a good one. "I should have stayed in bed."

"I agree, if all you're going to do is complain." She tapped the screen. "He's a possibility." The photo disappeared.

"It's a touch screen, so don't touch." I located the photo and made it full screen. The man had the right build and wore a baseball cap. Other than that, he could be anyone. The important clue was the fact he was at the community/campground lake picnic, which meant he'd been a resident of one of them. I knew for a fact he hadn't rented a tiny house.

I stood and retrieved the plastic bin from where I'd stashed it on top of my refrigerator. "Change up. We need to separate the men from the women campers. Disregard any that mention children." I set the bin on the table and moved the laptop to the kitchen counter.

"We need more room," Mags said. "Where can we go to find a larger table?"

"The library?" I finished coffee cup number one and poured another. "They don't open for a couple of hours."

She shook her head. "Since you're already being stalked, we need somewhere private."

"The chapel," we said in unison.

"There's a six-foot folding table in the storage room," I added. "Dress warm. It'll take a while for the place to heat up once we turn on the heater."

I put a knitted doggie sweater on Caper, filled a thermos with what remained of the hot coffee, and grabbed my coat. A few minutes later, we were zipping through the cold to the chapel I'd painstakingly restored as one of my first tasks to improve the community. We didn't have a regular pastor, but the place was always open for anyone needing peace and solitude, and sometimes the occasional homeless person stayed a while. As long as the place wasn't trashed, I didn't have a problem with overnight guests.

We shivered and shuffled through dry leaves and the five hundred feet to the chapel. With frigid fingers I unlocked the front door and rushed to turn on the heat before retrieving the table from the back room.

The soft hiss of the heater provided background to the shuffling of papers. Caper lay at my feet, head on her paws, eyes fixed on the door. Poor thing. She hated the cold.

By the time we warmed up, we had three stacks of papers in front of us. One were women campers, one small stack of family campers, and one stack of men.

"What's next?" Mags set the women and family piles back in the bin. "You do realize that just because the site was rented by a man doesn't mean it wasn't for a couple or a family, right?"

"I do." Now to figure out how to whittle the stack down further. "We could check social media? Did Mr. Robinson have a computer? We could try asking Parks and Recreation for more information, but since I'm a temporary employee, I doubt they'd tell us anything."

"They'd tell Davis."

"Yes, but he doesn't share info as well as I do." I drummed my fingers on the table. The proverbial light bulb clicked on over my head. "We'll call and say we're doing a survey asking what we can do to improve things and find out which sites were comprised of all men or families."

"That will take forever." Mags sagged in her chair. "I much prefer the pounding of pavement and peeking in windows. Spending hours on the phone is too much like a real job."

"I'm open to a better idea." I put an empty folder on top of the files in the bin, then added the rest. Spending a lot of time cold-calling wasn't my idea of fun either. To appease my friend, I suggested we take our morning trek around the campgrounds to see what we could see.

"How many baseball caps do you think the average redneck owns?" Mags asked as we hiked back to the golf cart.

"I have no idea. Why?"

"Because each time you've seen the suspects, you've described them wearing different caps. Do you think it's on purpose or do they match them to their outfits?"

I cast her a surprised look. "You think deer poachers care about whether or not their clothes match their caps?"

"Of course not, but if we could match a cap with a suspect, we might catch them." Her back stiffened and she marched ahead of me.

Loaded down with the bin of files, I struggled to catch up to her. "I didn't mean to offend you. The idea seemed a little silly to me."

"I've always been told no idea is a dumb idea."

"You're right. I'm sorry."

She stopped and faced me. "Robinson was my friend, too. I want to find who killed him as much as you do." Pain clouded her face.

"Is there something else bothering you?"

Her face fell. "I think Larry is seeing someone else."

"Why do you think that?" My heart fell. For as long as I'd known her, Mags had been searching for male companionship.

"He isn't over as much."

"Have you asked him why?"

She shook her head. "I don't want to seem

needy."

"Do you want me to talk to him?"

Her face brightened. "Would you? Thank you so much." She turned and headed back toward the cart, leaving me to wonder how in the world I could ask the uncle I barely knew whether he was cheating on my best friend.

We made the drive back to my place in silence. When we arrived, surprise filled me at the sight of Amber and Davis waiting at the picnic table in front of my house. Dread filled me. Had something happened to Eric? "Where is he?"

Davis held up a hand. "Eric is fine. We aren't here for anything bad."

"You found the bad guys?" Mags asked.

"No, I'm not here in any official capacity." He glanced at Amber and took her hand. "We're getting married, and Amber is moving in with me."

"When?" I scooped Caper into my arms.

"Today." Amber smiled up at Davis. "I've already packed. I hope you don't mind that I've put the house up for sale. There should be a sign by tomorrow."

"I don't, but we will miss you." Tears pricked my eyes. For years I'd had trouble making friends because of all the time required to care for Grams. Now, one of them was leaving. "When's the wedding?"

"We haven't set a date." Amber stepped forward and hugged me.

"Wait a minute." I stepped back and glared at Davis. "Eric said he was canoeing with you today."

Chapter Six

Davis's features darkened. "We finished by early afternoon."

With my heart in my throat, I pulled my cell phone from my pocket and turned to the tracking app. Eric's phone bleeped from the area of the river. "He's still there." Or at least his phone was. I held it up for the others to see. "We need to go." I headed for the house.

Davis shot out a hand to stop me. "It's dark, CJ. There's nothing you can do. Try calling him."

Duh. I called, but it went straight to Eric's voice mail. "Now what?"

Davis pressed his lips together, then glanced at Amber. "I've got to go."

She nodded. "Find Eric. I'll stay here with CJ."

"No, I'm going with Davis. You can stay with Mags." I glowered. No way would I be left behind.

He blew out his nose like a horse. "Fine. But do

as I say." He led the way to his car.

While we drove, I continued to call, text, and scream at my phone in vain attempts to get Eric to answer. "Is it possible he dropped his phone?"

"Of course it is." Davis cut me a quick glance. "We went to the parking lot together, discussed the fact we'd found no signs of the suspects camping along the river, and returned to our cars. When I drove off, he was still sitting there. I had no reason to assume he'd not left after me." He sounded defensive.

"I'm not blaming you." I groaned and rested my head against the back of the seat. Maybe I did blame him in some small way. He'd gone off and left my man behind.

"You're a terrible liar." A muscle ticked in his jaw.

I shrugged and stared out the window at the dark night, struggling to remain optimistic. "He's a park ranger, not a law enforcement officer."

"Your point?"

"You should have made sure he left the area."

"Yes, I should have. I'm sorry."

Nodding, I sniffed. "Love makes you forget things, focus only on that person. You had other things on your mind. Sometimes I forget you're human like the rest of us."

"Thank you, I think." He turned down a hard-packed dirt road that led to the river's parking lot.

When we reached it, Eric's vehicle was nowhere to be seen. I shoved open my door. "We need to find his phone."

"Hold up." Davis handed me a flashlight.

Leaving the car headlights on, we set off toward the trees, shining the flashlight beams back and forth in slow arcs.

I knew the phone tracker was accurate up to two-hundred feet. While I didn't relish going into the thick brush in the dark, it was too cold for snakes, and the light would dissuade any other creatures—two-legged or four—from harming me.

After an hour, Davis called it quits. "He isn't here."

"The tracker shows he is."

"His phone might be, but we've looked everywhere a man could be."

I narrowed my eyes. "Then look for the cellphone." I stepped over a log. Something crunched under my foot. I glanced down to see Eric's phone. "Found it and broke it." Tears obscured my vision and I plucked it out of the dirt. "He must have dropped it. Why and where is he now?"

"We'll find him. I just put out an APB on his jeep." Davis marched back to his car. "Come on. We won't locate him standing around an empty lot."

I jogged to the car and climbed into its warm interior. I hadn't realized how cold I'd become until I got inside. "We didn't see his vehicle on the way here, so let's try the opposite direction."

"Exactly my thought." He gave me a rare smile. "See? I told you you'd make a good cop."

"No, thanks. Too many rules and regulations." I grinned back. "I prefer skirting the line of the law."

"Too close sometimes." He turned right when we reached the main road.

"Wait, wait, wait." I pounded his arm. "There, in

the ditch." Dim rear lights cut through the dark. I was out of the car before Davis brought it to a complete halt.

Eric's jeep had crashed into a tree.

"Please, don't be dead." I cupped my hands around my eyes and peered through the driver's side window where Eric lay slumped over the wheel. Gripping the door handle with both hands, I yanked.

"Let me try." Davis pushed between me and the door. Inserting a crowbar in the space of the mangled door frame, he leaned against it. The door opened with a loud metallic screech. Davis reached in and checked for a pulse. "He's alive. Call for an ambulance."

"What mile marker are we at?" I dialed 9-1-1 and gave them the location Davis rattled off. Then I leaned against the jeep and kept my gaze locked on Eric's bloody face while we waited for help. When sirens wailed in the distance, I cried with relief.

Eric's eyes flickered open. "Hey."

"Hey," I swiped away my tears. "An ambulance is on its way."

"Good. I think my left arm is broken."

"Can you tell us what happened?" Davis leaned over.

"Can't it at least wait until he's been cared for?" I glared.

Davis held his hands up in surrender. "Fine. We'll follow him to the hospital."

"You can follow. I'm riding with him." And I did, watching over my man fall asleep again.

At the hospital, an orderly wheeled Eric to a curtained alcove, then out of my sight a few minutes earlier. By the time Davis arrived, I paced the small eight-foot section at least a dozen times.

"He's in X-ray," I said. "They're checking his head and his arm."

Davis ducked out, then returned with a Styrofoam cup of ice chips and water. "You look as if you need this." He handed it to me. "Sit down before the doctor gives you a tranquilizer."

"They'll do that?" My eyes widened, but I sat.

"Probably not, unless I tell them one is needed." His lips twitched.

Davis and I had never been enemies, but the fact we'd never been this cordial with each other before wasn't lost on me. No wonder Amber had fallen in love with the detective. He did have a heart beating under his muscled chest, and his handsome face could actually smile. No doubt she saw both on a regular basis. Of course, she didn't stop short of breaking the law on numerous occasions either.

I leaped to my feet when Eric was rolled back in, a cast on his arm. "You poor thing."

"Mr. Drake has a broken arm and a concussion. He refuses to be admitted to the hospital overnight. Is it possible for him to go home with one of you? We'd prefer he be supervised for twenty-four hours." The doctor glanced from me to Davis.

"He can stay with me." It wouldn't be the first time. In fact, Eric got injured a lot more now that we were dating than he had in his adult life.

Eric held out his hand. "This wasn't your fault."

How did he always know what I was thinking? I forced a smile and gave him a gentle kiss. "My sofa has a permanent indentation of your body."

At my house, Davis barely waited until Eric was settled before he rattled off questions. Eric held up his hand. "Whoa. I'll tell you what I can, which isn't much." He sat up while I plumped pillows behind him.

"I left the lot right after you did but turned right to patrol that length of road. Just when I'd decided the whole thing was a waste of time, a big Ford truck with deer antlers slammed me from behind."

"The suspects." I sat on the edge of the coffee table.

Eric nodded. "Best I could tell. Looked like the truck you've mentioned. Anyway, I increased my speed to get ahead of them to a place where I could safely turn around and head back toward town. I hadn't realized I'd lost my phone until then."

"Here it is." I handed it to him, shattered screen and all. "Sorry. I stepped on it."

He shook his head and dropped it on the sofa next to him. "Anyway, my jeep and the truck played a game of chase-and-slam for a while until one really hard hit sent me into the tree. That's all I remembered. I'm actually surprised to be alive. Why wouldn't they make sure they finished the job?"

"You looked dead to me," I said, shuddering. "You were barely recognizable under the blood."

"Good luck for me."

"Did you get a good look at who was in the truck?" Davis asked.

"No. There were two, but it was dark. No moon tonight." He lay back. "If I remember anything else, I'll give you a call."

"My cue to go." Davis heaved a sigh. "These men

are like the ghosts of a redneck winter. They come and go without a trace."

"Which means, they're somewhere close," Eric said. "We just have to find their hiding place. Don't worry. I'll find them."

"Not for a few days, you won't." I grabbed a folded afghan from a shelf over the sofa and covered him with it. "You're going to stay right here where I can take care of you."

"Nice of you to think so," he said with a smile. "You aren't the only stubborn person in the state of Arkansas."

"Unfortunately," Davis agreed, "that's true. Be careful, Drake. I'll do what I can on my end, but you know these mountains better than I do."

"Don't encourage him." I shooed Davis away and locked the door. If Eric tried to go back into the woods tomorrow, I'd be going with him. Of course, my Prius wouldn't be quite the same as a jeep with four-wheel drive.

I glanced at Eric to find him asleep. After letting Caper out for a quick break, I locked the door again and carried her upstairs. Wait. No one had been around all day to let Eric's dog, Hershey, out. I grabbed the spare key he'd given me a while back, shrugged into my coat, and rushed outside to my golf cart. Ten minutes later, I let a very happy chocolate lab outside to do his business. When Hershey finished, I took him to my place where he promptly licked Eric's hand and curled up on the floor next to the sofa.

Knowing that my family of sorts was safe for the time being, I climbed the stairs and went to bed.

Tomorrow would result in cold-calling a whole lot of people or driving into the woods in a hybrid car with Eric, or both of the above. I kind of hoped it would be cold-calling. My car wasn't made for adventure, and I wasn't keen on her getting scratched. I added talking to Larry to my mental to-do list. Tomorrow promised to be a very full day.

Chapter Seven

Eric groaned and struggled to sit up. I set down my coffee and rushed to help him. "Careful. That arm is going to hurt for a while." I propped pillows behind him. "Do you need a pain pill?"

"No, I need to get out there and find who killed Robinson and tried to kill me. Hand me my shoes."

"Well, I can't do that." I crossed my arms. "I can get you coffee, but you aren't going anywhere today."

He narrowed his eyes. "Let's not do this, CJ. You want to catch those people as much as I do."

"Yes, I do, but not at the expense of you." I filled a mug and handed it to him. "Mags and I are going to be calling everyone on that stack sitting in front of you. Maybe if you flipped through them, something might jump out at you. We could use your help with this and see how you feel tomorrow." I didn't want him to be angry with me, but I also didn't want him out there with killers when he wasn't feeling a hundred percent himself.

Eric's frown faded, replaced with a smile and a chuckle. "I forgot how bulldog you can be sometimes. Fine, I'll look through these papers. For what, exactly?"

"Anyone who's camped here and might be our deer killers." I grinned over the rim of my cup. We've already weeded out the sites registered under a woman's name, but may have to sort through them if we strike out here. I think we're safe setting families aside."

"I agree." His gaze met mine. "I'm not sure we're dealing with two men here."

"What?" My hand holding the cup froze halfway to the counter.

"I know it was dark and things happened pretty fast, but I'm not completely convinced that the passenger in the truck wasn't a woman."

I didn't like to stereotype, but it hadn't occurred to me that women could be poachers. "Great. Our workload just increased by half a ton." I plopped in the small chair across from him. Mags would not be thrilled. She hadn't wanted to make phone calls anyway.

A knock sounded at the door, sending Caper into her customary barking frenzy. From the rapid wag of her tail, someone she knew stood on the other side. I peered through the curtains to see Mags with a box of doughnuts in her hand.

I opened the door. "Yum."

"Good morning." She slapped away my hand when I reached for the box. "The patient gets first pick."

She held the box out to Eric, then set it on the coffee table.

I explained his theory that we might be searching for a man and a woman. "Sorry, but making the calls will take a lot longer. Eric will help us today."

"Have you mentioned it to Davis?" She asked Eric.

He shook his head. "I remembered it while sleeping, so it might be a dream, but something tells me it isn't." He bit into a chocolate cream-filled éclair. "I'll give you one day, CJ, of calling people, but tomorrow I'm back out there."

"In what vehicle?" Mags raised an eyebrow. "Your jeep is totaled."

He groaned and laid his head back. "Then a rental or my side-by-side."

"That won't be easy to drive with a broken arm." Mags was full of arguments this morning. At least Eric would be irritated with her and not me. She turned her attention on me. "Did you do what I asked you to?"

"When did I have time? After finding Eric, I went to the hospital, then here. I'll do it, but I don't think you have anything to worry about." That wasn't entirely true. I didn't know my uncle well enough to know whether or not he'd cheat on his girlfriend.

"I'm too old to go through this." She marched to my tiny galley kitchen and fixed a cup of coffee.

"What's going on?" Eric glanced from her to me.

"Larry has been MIA a lot. She wants me to grill him."

Eric laughed. "I can answer that, Mags. He's

volunteering at the local Boys and Girls Club repainting the gymnasium."

She whirled to face him. "Then why didn't he tell me so?"

Shrugging, Eric took another bite of his doughnut. "He's been a single man for a long time. Maybe it didn't occur to him."

"That's no excuse." The worry lines eased on her forehead. "If it isn't a secret, I'll cook him a special supper and ask him about it."

"It's not a secret."

It didn't take but a few minutes of calling to realize that a house of only three-hundred square feet did not make it easy for three people to talk and hear the people on the other line. I ended up going upstairs while Mags shut herself in the closet-sized bathroom.

I dialed my fifth number of the day and hoped someone would be home to answer. Maybe it would be more productive to call in the evenings or on the weekend. "Good morning, Mr. Oglesby. I'm calling on behalf of Blue Lake Campgrounds. We're taking a survey on how pleased you were with your experience and whether you had suggestions on improvement. Do you have a few minutes to help me?"

"Sweetheart, I'm retired. I have all the time you need." He chuckled. "The wife and I enjoyed our camping experience for the most part. What we didn't like was all the comings and goings all hours of the night."

I glanced at the dates on his reservation. Three weeks ago, right before the weather turned cold. Since the camp curfew was ten o'clock, I needed more information. "What sort of activity, sir? We strive to provide a pleasant experience."

"Revving of engines, loud talking—"

"Did you catch what they were talking about?" My breath caught. Had we caught a lucky break?

"This sounds more like an interrogation than a survey."

"I'm sorry. You aren't the only one we've received complaints from, and we'd really like to narrow this down and restrict further reservations of that party." I couldn't believe how easily persuasive words dripped from my tongue. Maybe I'd make good law enforcement like Davis said.

"They talked about some kind of hunting competition. Something about money for the biggest buck or some such foolishness. The more beer they drank, the louder they got."

"Thank you. You have been very helpful." I grinned and hung up the phone, glancing at the site number on his reservation sheet. He'd been in 105 which meant 103…I flipped through the pages…had been reserved by a Mr. and Mrs. Jones. I doubted that was their real name.

I called Mr. Oglesby back. "One more question, sir, if I may. Were the occupants of site 103 male or female?"

"One of each."

I hung up and thundered down the stairs. "Any luck?"

"I spoke with a woman who complained about a couple drinking and being loud a few weeks back," Mags said.

"Same here," Eric added, "but it was back in the

summer. You?"

"Site 103 and Mr. and Mrs. Jones." I grinned. "Want to bet that's a fake name?"

"Then how do we find them?" Mags asked, crossing her arms.

I shrugged, refusing to be deterred. "We go to the address listed, ask some questions, have Davis look up the driver's license numbers...we have a few things to go on. Eric, you need to check on the hunting competition Mr. Oglesby spoke about."

"It's something that's done every five years or so." He frowned. "It sounds as if our suspects are either thinning out to lessen the competition or taking antlers to keep in hopes of having one that beats out the competition. Either way, it's illegal and against the competition rules."

"How much does this thing pay?" Mags asked.

"First place is a thousand dollars."

"A lot of money but not worth going to jail for." I grabbed a glazed twisted doughnut from the box, surprised to see both eclairs gone. Eric's appetite hadn't failed him, it seemed. "Thanks for saving me something."

"You're welcome." He grinned and set his papers on the table. "I'm glad we didn't have to go through them all. Talk about boring. Let's call Davis with the news."

Davis was at Amber's, so he arrived on my doorstep within ten minutes. "Good job, you three." He held out his hand for the paper.

"You already have a copy," I told him. "Remember?"

He tilted his head. "CJ."

"Ugh." I snapped a picture with my phone and gave him a look that dared him to say anything. "We do the work and you get the glory."

He rolled his eyes. "Don't give me that. You've been in the newspaper plenty of times for your moments of fame."

"That's my cue to skedaddle." Mags waved her fingers and hurried out the door.

Traitor. "How are you going to find out who they really are?"

"Maybe they are Mr. and Mrs. Jones." He shook his head. "Don't borrow trouble. You trip over it too much as it is." He folded the paper and stuck it in his pocket. "Eric, hurry up and get that cast off. I'd like you to be my best man." He flashed a grin and dashed out the door.

"I'm honored, but would've liked the opportunity to answer." Eric grinned and spread out on the sofa. "I'm going to catch a few winks. Stay out of trouble, sweetheart."

Even I could manage that for an hour or two. I clipped Caper's leash on her collar and locked the door behind me as I left to make my rounds. At Amber's place, number four, she'd already packed her few things into a small U-Haul.

"Hey, CJ. Want to be my maid of honor?" She glanced up from putting a box into the trailer.

"I'd love to." My heart swelled. "I'm going to miss having you around."

"Oh, I'll be here visiting Mags on regular occasions. I've found a buyer for my house."

"That was fast." *Please, God, don't let her house turn into a cursed place like number ten.* "Who is it?"

"A newly married couple from Maine. They came by yesterday and paid cash. You'll like them. They're adorable." She closed the door to the trailer. "That's it. Climb off that cart and give me a hug."

I hurried to oblige. "When do you want to start planning the wedding?"

"Next week. Bill and I are going out of town for the weekend to scout out a place for our honeymoon. I'm thinking I'd like to stay in the state and maybe go to Eureka Springs."

I stepped back. "That isn't very far."

"No, but come springtime or fall, it's gorgeous." She grinned and jogged to her car. "Ciao."

I sighed, missing her already. She didn't get involved in my adventures, but she did have a talent for talking me out of dangerous situations. A nice contrast to her grandmother's encouragement. Since her house wasn't a rental, my job there was done. I returned to the cart and Caper and continued down the road.

Roy fiddled with the motor of his cart, so I stopped. "What's up?"

"Dead battery." He wiped his hands on an oily cloth. "I have another one in storage if you wouldn't mind giving me a ride on this chilly morning."

"Sure, hop in." Once he got settled, I asked, "You look like a hunting man. Are you?"

"When I can. Having a passel of kids doesn't leave me with a lot of free time. Why?"

"I thought that would be your break away." I smiled. "Know anything about the competition this year?"

"Only that I've always wanted to join. I could use

the prize money."

I told him about the man and woman we were on the lookout for. "How do you feel about going undercover and entering? I'll pay the entrance fee."

"CJ, if you give me the time off, I'll be glad to pay my own fee." His broad face split in a grin. "Let me warn you, though. If I wind up dead, my wife will kill you."

"Then, please stay alive." I laughed and sped toward the storage shed, hoping Roy knew where the big bucks were hiding. If he won, not only would he have the prize money, but we'd have dealt a little more justice to people who thought cheating and murder were the way to win.

Chapter Eight

"I'm not crazy about this," Roy's wife, Tammy, said later that morning. "There will be people with guns in the woods."

"That's part of hunting, dear." Roy cast me a frustrated look. "I told you she wouldn't be keen on the idea."

"I need his help, Tammy. He'll be wearing his orange hat and vest. It's regulation." I gave her the most reassuring grin I could. "If I could go in his place, I would."

"Send Mags's man."

Good idea. It wouldn't hurt to have two so-called spies out there. "I will, but please reconsider Roy going." I kept my smile in place until I reached the cart. Larry would do it without a second thought, so at least I'd have someone out there. I couldn't believe I hadn't thought of him myself.

None of the residents of Heavenly Acres were

stirring that cold October morning so I drove to Mags's where I hoped Larry would be. I didn't see his truck, which meant he would most likely be at the Boys and Girls Club. If Eric felt up to it, we could make the drive into town. I needed a few groceries anyway.

When I arrived home, Eric sat on my front steps, a jacket flung over his shoulder and a cup of coffee in his right hand. "I can fend for myself since it's the left arm that's broken," he said with a grin.

"I like taking care of you." I gave him a kiss, then sat next to him while keeping an eye on Caper. "Feel like going to town?"

"Definitely. Since my nap, I'm going stir-crazy."

"After less than an hour?" I tilted my head. "You're in trouble then." I stood and went to retrieve my shopping list from off the fridge. By the time I'd turned around, Eric had Caper safely in the house and waited by the door.

"I'm ready." I locked the door behind us and headed for the Prius. "Are you wanting to stop at the rental-car place?"

Eric nodded. "I need a four-wheel drive but not sure they'll have something like that. My insurance will cover a standard sedan, so hopefully an upgrade won't break the budget."

Unfortunately the lack of four-wheel drive vehicles to rent didn't bode well for the rest of our day. Eric declined a sedan, muttering he'd stick with his side-by-side until he received the insurance money toward a new vehicle.

I chalked his poor attitude to pain and headed for the community center. Sure enough, Larry stood halfway up a ten-foot ladder with a paintbrush in his hand.

"Hey." I said, putting a hand on the ladder.

He jerked, getting navy-blue paint on the ceiling. "Don't sneak up on me like that, girl." He glared down at us, removing an ear bud. "I could have fallen and broken my neck." Climbing down, he swiped his hand across his coveralls. "What's up?"

"First, I didn't mean to scare you. Second, I have a favor." I smiled.

"What happened, Ranger?" Larry stepped past me. "My niece beating you up?"

I crossed my arms. "When was the last time you spoke with Mags? If you had recently, you'd know how Eric got his arm broken."

A sheepish look crossed my uncle's face. "Hey, Charlie, I'm taking a break."

"It's good." A man in his thirties waved a hand in our direction, then pushed a flatbed dolly through an open door.

"He's alright but a bit grumpy most of the time," Larry explained as he led us to a break room.

"We need somewhere more private," I told him. "Can you leave?"

"Since I'm a volunteer, I can do whatever I want." He stripped off his coverall, revealing a flannel shirt and jeans. "Let's grab lunch. I'll buy."

He squeezed into the backseat of my car and directed us to a diner famous for its southern food. We asked the hostess for a table as far away from the other tables as possible and slid into a corner booth.

"What's up with all the cloak and dagger?" Larry said, grinning.

"First, I need to know why you're avoiding Mags?" I sharpened my look. "She thought at first you were cheating on her."

He put a hand to his chest. "I'd never do that."

"Then why haven't you told her what you do all day?" I leaned my elbows on the table. "You say you love her."

"I do. That's the problem." He rubbed both hands vigorously down his face. "I need to think about whether I have what it takes to commit to a future with her. That's why I'm painting the walls of the community building. It helps me think."

"She still deserves to know." I smiled, reassured that all would be fine between the two of them. A man who agonized over a woman this way was alright.

"Can one of you talk to her?" He glanced from me to Eric.

"No way." Eric shook his head. "You'll have to man up and face the tiger of Heavenly Acres yourself."

Larry sighed. "She'll bite me."

"Don't be ridiculous." I browsed my menu. "Eric, tell this scaredy-cat how you got hurt." *Yum, chicken fried steak and potatoes with gravy.*

When Eric finished, Larry straightened against the back of the booth. "Dude, that could've been fatal."

"Yep, which leads to CJ's favor." Eric motioned toward me.

I waited until the waitress took our order, then asked, "How do you feel about hunting?"

"If it isn't for sport, I enjoy it. Why?"

I told him about the poachers, the truck that kept showing up, and the competition. As I talked, his expression grew graver.

"So, you want me to go into the woods with someone who will want to kill me if they find out why I'm really there?" His brow furrowed.

"That's what Tammy Olson said about Roy." I sighed. "You'd be there to hunt deer. Finding news on the poachers is a bonus."

He reached across the table and put his hand on mine. "I didn't say I wouldn't do it, honey. I will. I've the background for it, so I'll know danger when it faces me."

"Thank you." I grinned. "I'm still trying to convince Roy because he knows a lot of the folks around here."

Eric chuckled. "If you want to make CJ happy, all you have to do is say yes to whatever she wants."

I joined in the laughter. "What can I say? I'm easy to read."

After lunch, we dropped Larry off to paint for a few more hours. As I circled the car to leave, Mags drove up. "Uh-oh."

She narrowed her eyes and rolled down her window. "Why didn't you invite me to lunch with the three of you? I brought Larry lunch only to be told he'd left."

"Spur of the moment," Eric said, leaning around me. "We didn't plan to exclude you."

Tears shimmered in her eyes. "Well, that's what happened." She glanced toward the building where Larry stood watching, dressed again in paint-splattered coveralls. "Isn't he fine-looking?"

"Go talk to him," I said. "We'll catch up to you later. Oh, and please do not talk him out of hunting."

Her eyes widened. "Why would I do that? I love venison." Shaking her head, she parked.

"You might think I'm easy to read," I told Eric, "but that woman is the complete opposite."

By the time we arrived at the grocery store, pained lines marred his features.

"Are you sure you feel up to this?"

"It isn't my legs that are broken." He shoved open the passenger side door.

"I don't want you overdoing things. The accident was less than forty-eight hours ago."

"I'm fine." He forced a smile and waved his good arm for me to go ahead of him into the store. "Although, I'll let you push the cart."

"Gladly." I led the way to health and beauty, leaving Eric to sit while I browsed the aisle looking for the exact brand of shampoo I liked. When I returned, he was deep in conversation with Charlie from the community center.

The man's gaze hardened when it landed on me. "Ma'am."

I frowned. "Hello."

"Charlie is just picking up a few things before he heads home," Eric said with an expression that said to be nice.

Why wouldn't I be nice? Other than being unfriendly, the man hadn't done anything to me. "I'll meet you by the paper products." Head high, back straight, I marched away. Except for those who wanted to hurt me, most people liked me. If I'd given a strange look, it was only because I was taken back by the man's unfriendly glare. I tossed a package of napkins into the cart. Anyone would have made a face at that.

"Are you upset?" Eric peered around the corner of a stack of toilet paper.

"A little." I narrowed my eyes. "Why the look?"

"I didn't want you to run him off. Charlie is an avid hunter, I found out, so I asked him a few questions about the local hunting community." He approached the cart slowly as if I were a wild animal preparing to pounce. Or Mags.

"Did you learn anything?"

"Not really. He doesn't know anyone with antlers on their truck. Said lots of people have them in their homes, though."

I nodded. "That doesn't help much."

"Sorry, babe." He gave me a one-armed hug. "Let's finish shopping and figure out the next step."

I couldn't agree more. Grocery shopping was not my favorite pastime.

We finished the list, paid for our purchases and loaded them into the trunk of my car. As I turned to move to the driver's side, I spotted the truck with the antlers. "Eric."

He glanced where I pointed. "I can't believe the very people we're looking for are here."

"How do we figure out who?" I tried to make out the license plate number under a thick splatter of mud.

"We wait."

"I've got meat in the trunk." I sighed and climbed in the car. With nothing frozen, I hoped the cold temperatures would keep my purchases from spoiling.

After an hour, my bladder needed emptying and my stomach needed filling. Eric had fallen asleep in the passenger seat. Trying not to wake him, I jogged into the store and into the restroom.

Happy to see the truck still parked in the lot, I opened my trunk to pull out a bag of chips I'd bought. I checked the meat and vegetables to make sure they'd stayed cold and stepped back to close the trunk.

Something hit me in the back of the head and my world went dark.

Chapter Nine

I didn't think I was out for long, but when I woke up, I was in the tiny trunk of my car. Eric!

Banging and yelling would surely attract the attention of someone, anyone. What had they done with Eric? He was in no condition to fight. Asleep in the front passenger seat, he'd be no deterrent to someone wanting to hurt him. I screamed and banged louder.

The trunk opened, and I blinked into the confused face of Eric. "What? Why are you in the trunk?"

I held up my hand. "Don't ask questions. Help me out. Is that truck still here? Someone hit me in the back of the head." I put a hand to the throbbing spot and brought away fingers sticky with blood. "I'm getting woozy."

"You don't faint at the sight of blood, CJ." Eric put his arm around me and led me to the passenger side of the car. "It's most likely the hit to the head that's made you dizzy. Let me look." He tenderly probed under my hair. "Not too deep. You'll have a headache but nothing more serious. I'll drive us home." His lips curled. "Some of your groceries are a bit smooshed."

"We'll worry about that later." I clicked my seatbelt into place, vowing to get even with whoever sucker punched me. If the grave expression on Eric's face was any indication, he felt the same. "At least we know with certainty that the deer-truck owners are the guilty ones."

"Not necessarily." Eric backed from the spot using only one arm. "Could be coincidence."

"You don't believe that." I frowned, rolling my eyes toward him since moving my head hurt too much.

He sighed. "No, I don't. They are definitely involved. With them running me off the road and you getting hit when the truck sat in the same lot…yeah."

"Nothing wrong with wishful thinking." I wished I'd gotten the license plate. We weren't any further along in our investigation than we were before. Glancing in the sideview mirror, I couldn't help but feel relieved not to see the truck following us. Neither of us were in any condition for a confrontation.

"Wake up." Eric wiggled the steering wheel, sending my Prius weaving. "No sleeping after a head injury."

Ugh. I fought to keep my eyes open as we pulled alongside my house. I got halfway to my steps before remembering the groceries. Sighing, I joined Eric in front of my open trunk. Half the carton of eggs were broken and a loaf of bread smashed, but other than a few other items with dented corners, I hadn't done too much damage lying on my purchases. I loaded my arms with bags and shuffled toward the house.

By the time I put everything away, Eric and I crashed on the sofa. I snuggled under his good arm and closed my eyes, ignoring his whispered demand that I stay awake.

"CJ."

I opened my eyes to see Amber and Davis leaning over me. "What?"

"Amber is going to look at you while I question Eric." Davis's worried gaze let me know he actually did care about me. "Oh, and I want you to call Ann to come watch over you."

Poor thing. Being my bodyguard always brought trouble to the one assigned that task. I nodded and let Amber shine a light in my eyes. Then she probed the sore spot on my head.

"Let me put some antiseptic on this. It'll burn." She poured some smelly liquid onto a cloth and pressed it to my wound. "It isn't bad, but you do have a concussion. I can call someone to get you a prescription for pain meds, but I'd really like you to stay awake."

"She's already slept an hour," Eric said. "I tried to keep her awake. That's why I called you."

"You should have taken her to the ER." Amber narrowed her eyes in his direction.

"Don't be mad at Eric for knowing I'd refuse to go." I scooted to a more comfortable position. "I can also answer questions in regard to what happened to me."

"Fine." Davis pulled a foldable chair from a hook on the wall and sat down to face me. "Tell me what happened."

"Eric and I spotted the truck in the parking lot and decided to stay and see who owned it. Except—" I grinned sheepishly, "—when Eric fell asleep, I locked the car doors and ran to the restroom. When I came back out, the truck was still there. I opened my trunk to get some chips and…someone hit me. I don't know how long I was in there before I woke up and started yelling."

Davis glanced at Eric. "How long?"

He shrugged. "The pain meds knocked me out. I promise I will not be taking them anymore. Too dangerous. CJ could have been killed."

"They could have killed you, too." I motioned for him to come sit with me. "I promise to call Ann as soon as the two of you leave. There isn't enough room in here for another person."

David stood. "Then, we'll get out of here. I've put out an APB on a truck with antlers, but no one other than the two of you have spotted it. Don't go anywhere alone. Either of you."

"Not going to happen." Eric shook his head. "I've got a job to do and will be back to work tomorrow."

Davis opened his mouth to say something, then snapped it shut. "Stubborn people."

Amber smiled. "Please don't wait to call the next time one of you get hurt. Don't protest either." She held up a hand to halt the argument coming from me. "We all know it's a matter of time." She linked her arm with Davis's and they left.

Eric pushed to his feet and locked the door. "Call

Ann."

"Um, where's my dog?" I glanced under the coffee table where she usually lay. Instead, Hershey chewed on one of my gym shoes, then glanced up at me with big innocent eyes. "She must have snuck out when Amber and Davis arrived."

Eric opened the front door and whistled. "Caper." He turned a worried expression on me. "I don't see her." Hershey tried to streak past him, only to be stopped by Eric's quick grab of his collar.

"That dog and her wandering." I climbed to my feet and stepped outside. "Caper, come get a treat." Spotting her leash still attached to the tethered line in my yard, I glanced at Eric. "Did you put her there when we got home?"

He shook his head. "I don't remember seeing her when we brought in the groceries."

Neither had I, come to think of it. The last time I'd let her out was first thing that morning, and I had definitely returned her to the house. "I don't remember if I unlocked the door when we got home." I'd carried the groceries inside. Right. I hadn't had to set them down. "My door was unlocked. I'm certain of it."

"Did you lock it when we left?"

"I always do, but now I'm not sure." Still, my little dog couldn't open doors; neither could Hershey. "She has to be inside the house."

There weren't that many places for a dog to hide. Caper also wasn't frightened of many things. If she were somewhere she couldn't get out, someone put her there.

I started opening the few kitchen cabinets I had.

She lay curled up in the galvanized tub that made up the floor of my shower. She didn't respond to being picked up and a rolled sheet of paper stuck out of her collar.

"Eric." Sobs stuck in my throat.

He took one look at her, said we needed to get to the vet, and had me running out the door to the car. I removed the paper and shoved it into my pocket.

Twenty minutes later, Caper lay on an examining table while a veterinarian checked her over. "I'll do bloodwork," he said, "but my guess is someone gave her a sleeping pill. A dangerous thing to do with a dog this small. I'd like to keep her overnight so we can keep an eye on her."

Blinking back tears, I nodded. "Anything that will help her. So, she'll be alright?"

He smiled. "I think so. Give us a call in the morning to see if she's ready to go home."

With Eric's hand on the small of my back, we returned to the car. I pulled the paper from my pocket and read it out loud, "This time is a warning. Stay out of the competition. Stop trying to find us. Next time, your dog won't only be sleeping, and you'll get something worse than a hit on the head." We really needed to train Hershey to be more protective.

I swallowed past the lump in my throat. "Rather than call Ann, let's see if she's home." My Grams's house was less than five minutes from where we were.

Now that Eric had driven with one arm and we were still alive, he insisted on driving all the time. I didn't care. My thoughts were on poor Caper.

When we pulled into the driveway, Ann turned,

water hose in hand. She grinned, waved, and turned off the water. "Haven't seen you two in a while. Looks like you've had some adventure." Her gaze landed on the cast on Eric's arm. "From the serious expressions on your faces, I gather this isn't a social call."

"Sorry," Eric said. "Can we talk inside?"

"Sure. Come on in. I've got tea."

While we settled ourselves on her dark brown leather sofa, she headed to the kitchen. Other than the floor plan, Grams's house seemed different with furniture not stuck in the sixties. I didn't think Ann would renovate countertops or appliances since she only rented, but I knew it needed to be done soon if I decided to sell.

She carried in a tray with a pitcher, three cups, and a sugar jar. She set the tray on a glass-topped coffee table. "Pour and shoot." What I liked to call her cop face settled into place. A look that showed she meant business.

I explained about finding Mr. Robinson, Eric told about the deer poaching, and we took turns telling the rest.

"Point is," I added, "Davis told me to hire you to watch over me."

Ann sat straight in her chair, her gaze locked on mine. "Can't you stay out of danger for more than three months?"

"Obviously not." I smirked. "It's like a cloud following me around, hovering over my head."

"Lucky for you, I'm not on a current job." She leaned forward, elbows on her knees. "You're the only one that requires I move in. I like this house, CJ.

I feel like I'm living in a box in yours. Still, we're friends, so I'm willing to compromise."

"Does that mean you'll watch over me for free?" I grinned.

"Nope." She smiled. "You'll get a discount, but I need some kind of compensation for the dangers I'll face protecting you." Which meant she wouldn't pay rent for as long as she was my protector. "I'll go pack a bag and grab Sprinkles. Enjoy your tea."

Sprinkles? Something rubbed my ankle. I glanced down to see a gray tabby kitten. Ah. Ann had gotten a cat. Caper would not be pleased.

A few minutes later, Ann placed a large duffel bag next to the door, slid the kitten into a padded pet carrier, and cleaned up the tea items. When she returned, she rubbed her hands together. "Let's catch us some deer killers."

"Protection is what you're hired for," Eric said, laughing. "Don't encourage CJ to keep investigating."

She raised her eyebrows. "I'm a private investigator slash bodyguard slash whatever I'm needed to be. I'm not stupid enough to believe CJ will be content to stay locked in her house. We've all been there, done that, and learned otherwise. Besides, I don't like anyone who harms animals for sport, meanness, or vengeance."

Neither did I. "Let's do this."

Chapter Ten

When I woke up the next morning, Ann and Eric had devised a diabolical plot without me. Eric would continue to sleep on my sofa while Ann would sleep in the loft with me. That made three adults, one large dog, one small dog, and a rambunctious kitten in my three-hundred square-foot home.

"Strength in numbers," Ann said when I complained. "Eric isn't safe at home alone any more than you are."

That comment stopped my argument cold. "You're right. If I didn't have to patrol the campgrounds and the community, I'd suggest we move into Grams's place for the time being." But that would be a lot of running back and forth, and one of the stipulations of my job was that I live onsite.

"We'll manage, sweetheart." Eric gave me a lingering kiss full of promise, then clipped a leash to Hershey's collar. "I'll be gone most of the day which will give you some space. I'll take the big galoot here with me."

"I don't want you to go." Fear threatened to choke me. "You'll be a sitting duck."

"I can't live in fear. You know that."

I did. I'd said the same thing more than once. "Be careful. You don't have an Ann."

He chuckled. "Stay safe, sweetheart."

"There's only one of me," Ann said, locking the door after him. "Coffee, then pick up Caper?"

"We'll take the coffee with us." I clomped my way upstairs, kicking aside dog-chew toys—Hershey's work. Somebody could fall and break their neck.

The receptionist at the vet's office greeted us with a smile. "Caper is doing great. She's such a little darling." She slid the bill across the counter.

I glanced at the total, sighed, and handed over my credit card. Pet bills were almost as high as human bills. After I paid, the woman led me to a small room to wait for my dog. Ann elected to stay in the waiting room to make a few phone calls. I'd have her fill me in later. Right now, I wanted my puppy.

"Here she is, Miss Turley." The vet entered the room and handed me a squirming Caper.

I held her close and nuzzled my face in her fur. "Thank you so much."

The vet's expression grew grave. "It's a wise idea to keep toxic chemicals out of her reach. That includes medications."

"I didn't give them to her, and the police have been notified. Thank you." I frowned and joined Ann outside on the sidewalk. It rankled me that anyone would think I'd be careless in leaving medication where a curious dog could get into them.

"What's wrong?" Ann disconnected from whomever she'd been talking to and slipped her phone into her pocket.

"The vet insinuated I'd left medicine out." I marched for my car.

"He's only concerned for his patient."

"Whatever." I set Caper in the backseat. When I straightened, I caught sight of a set of antlers sticking around the side of the building. "There's the truck." I slammed the Prius door and took off at a sprint toward the vehicle. When I got my hands on them...

The truck's engine roared to life. The vehicle rocketed toward me.

Stupid move on my part. I leaped over a flower planter and rolled close to the nearest store door.

Ann darted past me, took a stance, and aimed her gun at the truck. It didn't deter the driver. Instead he, or she, kept coming, and Ann joined me on the sidewalk. She rubbed her shoulder and glared at me as the truck sped away. "Don't ever do something that stupid again."

"I acted without thinking." I groaned, pushing to my feet. I'd sport some colorful bruises come morning. "Tell me you noted the license plate numbers."

"Too muddy."

"What we need is a good hard rain." I limped back to the Prius. When I spotted the truck at a traffic light, I increased my speed. "Come on. We'll follow them."

"In this thing?" Ann's brow wrinkled. "I guess

we can try. I should have brought my Mustang."

"You have a Mustang?" My eyes widened. "Well, yeah, you should have brought it." Duh. I climbed into the driver's seat.

"I didn't want anything to happen to it. It's only a month old." She clicked her seatbelt into place. I pulled two cars behind the truck at the light. The only thing good about my car following another was the small size allowed me to hide behind larger vehicles.

"I guess it's no secret I've hired a bodyguard." I sent a quick grin Ann's way. "You were like Annie Oakley back there."

She chuckled. "Just keep your eyes on the road." She typed a number on her phone. "Davis, this is Ann Lowery. CJ and I are in pursuit of suspect. Headed for I-40. Keep the tracker on her phone." She listened for a minute, then scowled. "Because they tried to run us over at the vet's. Gee." She hung up and shook her head. "He wanted to know why we were pursuing. Isn't it self-explanatory?"

"To me, it is." When Ann had been a cop under Davis, she would never have considered a car chase with me. She'd have insisted I go home, lock the door, and stay hidden while letting the police do their job. I liked the new Ann much better.

Caper whined and slid to the floor as I veered toward the exit onto the Interstate at a fast clip. "Sorry, girl." I needed to buy her one of those doggie seatbelts. For now, she was safer on the floor.

"There." Ann pointed to the truck whipping around a motorhome. "You're going to lose him."

Eventually, yep. I pressed the accelerator harder, sending my engine humming. The truck continued to pull ahead. When it veered onto an exit ramp and left the Interstate, I followed. When it shot down a side road, I stopped. "They want us to follow."

"It's beginning to appear that way."

"I'm not that stupid. Make note of where we are and send the location to Davis." I turned the car around and headed home. What a waste of time. One of these days, I'd come face-to-face with whoever tried to harm Caper and I'd make them pay. I didn't know how, but I had time to come up with something ugly, something bad.

"I know you're angry," Ann said, "but you might want to slow down before you wreck the car and kill us."

"Oh. Right." I'd pushed the car to ninety. I slowed to just a few miles over the speed limit and wondered how Eric's day was going. Safely, I hoped.

At the house, we traded the car for the golf cart and headed for the campgrounds. Caper sat up, tail wagging between us. I patted her head, thankful she didn't appear any the worse from her ordeal.

"Have you considered putting plastic around this cart to keep the cold out?" Ann pulled her jacket tighter around her. "Or buy one with a removable top and a heater?"

"You get used to it." I grinned and kept going.

The crime-scene tape had fallen down around Robinson's camper. The site brought back the sadness of finding his body, and the suspicion which rose at the site of deer meat in his cooler. I didn't think Robinson could be a poacher, but the meat didn't lie. I could only hope he'd stolen it from the bad guys.

I sighed and headed to the rack set up for skinning deer. A young man worked on a carcass. I didn't care to see whether buck or doe. Deer season had started, and I didn't care. "Nice one."

"Thanks." He barely glanced at us.

"Are you entered into the competition?"

He shook his head. "I wanted to, but putting meat on the table is more important than a trophy."

"The prize money is good."

"Look, lady, this deer isn't going to prepare itself." He glowered. "Besides, if you saw how many are out in those woods, armed to the teeth, you'd think twice about going anywhere near them."

I glanced at Ann. "Maybe we should see how many men are registered for the competition." I doubted whether our suspects had. They seemed to prefer doing things illegally. "Eric is going to need help while this is going on."

"It won't be us. I don't know anything about hunting."

I thanked the young man for his time and headed for Heavenly Acres. Tammy strolled down the side of the road, a bag of garbage in her hand. "Roy off hunting?"

She nodded. "And I'm left holding the bag. Literally. Danny can help, but not until he gets home from school. How long does this thing last?"

"A week, I think."

She groaned and continued toward the dumpster, muttering about men getting to play while women had to stay home and do all the work. I felt guilty. I'd been so concerned with my own problems and hadn't considered hers.

"I'll take care of the public trashcans until Roy returns," I told her.

"That would be a big help, CJ. Thank you." She gave a nod and headed home.

"I'm not going dumpster diving," Ann said once the other woman had passed. "Neither are you. The last time you did, I swore you'd never get the stink out."

I'd fallen into discarded roadkill while looking for evidence. I agreed with Ann about staying out of dumpsters.

Mags stepped onto her porch and shook out an area rug. Dust rose, then fell to her dormant flowerbed. She waved us over.

Uh-oh. We'd left her out again.

"I see Ann is back." Mags pressed her lips together.

"Someone gave Caper sleeping pills," I told her. "Eric and Davis thought it wise."

Mags nodded, glancing toward the mountain. In the distance we heard the occasional gunshot. "I can't wait until this week is over."

I hoped the end of the week would have the poachers behind bars. "Did you get everything straightened out with Larry?"

"Oh, yes. He admitted to being afraid of commitment. I took that as a challenge to show him that I am not a woman he wants to get away." Her eyes sparkled. "I'm going to love that man and shower him with so much affection, he'll be dumbfounded."

"Does that mean you aren't going to get in our way?" Ann arched a brow.

Mags glared. "I never get in the way. Do I plan on continuing to help CJ? Most definitely." She gave the rug a hard flap in our direction.

Ann sneezed. "Same ole Mags."

"Same ole Ann."

I rolled my eyes, then told Mags of our experiences that morning. "I really don't have a plan as to what to do next."

"I do." Mags opened her door, set the rug on the floor inside, then closed the door. "You need to go up on that mountain."

"But Larry and Roy are up there. What can I do?"

"You've seen more of the poachers than they have. If you could lay eyes on one of them, you might recognize them from the photos. In fact, I picked up some orange hats and vests this morning. I was going to bring them by in a little while." Mags said.

I didn't know what to say and met Ann's shocked gaze. Mags was serious. She expected us to go hunting.

Chapter Eleven

Mags eyed the outfit I'd picked for our romp through the forest. "You cannot wear hot pink."

"I hate orange, especially that shade." I made a face at the hunting vest and cap in her hands. "This pink will definitely show I'm not a deer."

"How many women do you think are on that mountain?" She put her hands on her hips and raised her eyebrows.

"Considering what century we live in, I'd say quite a few."

"Not as many as you'd think. I suggest we try to look as much like men or boys as we can." She thrust the vest at me. "Change your clothes. We should be up there before the sun comes up. The guns are in the car. Where's Ann?"

I hated guns. Mags knew that. I'd told her more than once about my cousin dying in a drive-by shooting which had been at the wrong house, wrong target. "I won't carry a gun, and Ann left during the night. Said she had a lead."

"Oh, stop. Yours is only a pellet gun." She rolled her eyes. "Lock up Caper and let's go. I don't know why you let Ann go without you."

"Because that's what I hired her to do. Help find out who killed Robinson. I don't think she expected us to leave at the crack of dawn." I gave the dog a quick hug and locked the door behind me, leaving a disgruntled Caper inside. Spotting a four-wheeler, I asked, "Whose is that?"

"I borrowed it from a friend."

"Does this friend know you have it?" I quirked my mouth.

She grinned. "Larry will know as soon as he gets home. He won't miss it. The man owns two of them and is using the other one. I figured we could borrow this."

She had a strange sense of logic.

"I'm driving." I climbed in front, leaving her to climb behind me after securing the guns to the rack in the back. "Where to?"

"Oh, right. Here." She handed me her phone. "I put a tracker thingy on Larry's phone. Head for that dot, but don't get too close. I haven't told him yet."

"Wow, you're turning into a regular criminal." I secured the phone in a cup holder next to me and lurched forward and sped off. I felt a bit like an astronaut as the skin on my face rippled and my head tilted back.

Mags yelped and somersaulted off the back. "Hey."

"Oh, my gosh." I let go of the handle and rushed

to her aid. "It's got more power than I thought. Are you okay?"

"Are you sure you can drive a four-wheeler?" She glared and pushed to her feet. "Because I'm not convinced."

"If I can drive a golf cart, I should be able to drive this." I frowned. "I'll be careful."

"Yes, please." She marched past me and resumed her seat, causing me to have to squeeze into place.

I deserved it. She could have been hurt by my foolishness. This time I turned the handle a lot slower and drove down the path past the chapel. Then I veered off the path and headed up the mountain toward the sound of gunshots.

We reached the mountain as the sun made its first peek over the top. "Where to now?" I stopped and glanced over my shoulder.

Mags climbed off. "We lock this baby to a tree and start walking."

I was afraid she'd say that. Sighing, I took the chain she handed me and secured our ride home. Mags handed me the pellet gun, which looked way too much like a real rifle, and we set off. My face already felt frozen from the four-wheeler ride, and it didn't take my feet long to feel the same. Why couldn't hunting be in the spring?

"Hold up." Mags gripped my arm. "There's a deer."

A splendid buck stood a few feet away, head high, ears alert for sound. I held my breath and stood still. When a shot rang out close by, I realized we could be standing in the path of a bullet. Someone would see this magnificent animal and shoot it.

I waved my arms. "Go. Shoo." The deer bounded away, and I pulled Mags down.

"I was going to shoot him." She pulled her arm free. "I bet I would've won the competition."

"You aren't registered." I glared at her. "Do you even have a license?" It occurred to me that I didn't. If we were caught, no one would believe we were up here with guns and not hunting.

"No, I don't. That's probably not a good thing."

I sighed. "Now what?"

"We scout around, and you study everyone we see. Something might jump out at you."

"That's what I'm afraid of," I muttered. "Something like a bullet."

"Stop being such a scaredy-cat." Mags slipped in front of me and led the way around a small clearing. "There." She pointed to where a man with an orange cap sat in front of a tree.

"He's in plain sight." I tilted my head.

"Deer aren't afraid unless you move. They're cute but not very bright. Does he look familiar?"

"No." The man we watched had shaggy grey hair and a beard. "We're looking for someone younger. The woman won't be far away, I'm guessing."

Someone cleared their throat behind us. I gasped and whirled. Mags lunged forward, Taser in hand.

Eric jerked and fell.

"Mags, you'd better run. That's the second time you've tased him." I bent over and stared into Eric's outraged face. "You'd better not have hurt his broken arm."

"He needs to stop sneaking up on me."

"I didn't know you had your Taser out." I

returned her glare.

"Of course, I did. You don't want me to shoot someone, do you?"

Well, no.

Eric groaned and climbed to his feet. "If you weren't a woman, I'd punch you in the face."

"I'm sorry." The grin on her face led me to believe otherwise.

"What are the two of you doing out here?" His gaze flicked the gun on my back. "Armed?"

"Mine isn't real. Are you okay?" I cupped his face.

He nodded. "Despite the attempts of Mags to hurt me."

"We're up here looking for the poachers." Mags crossed her arms. "Someone has to do something."

"Larry and I *are* doing something. Go home before I issue you both a ticket for not having a license."

My mouth fell open. Eric was acting a lot like Davis, and I didn't like it. "The more eyes the better. We thought if I saw the poachers, I might recognize something about them. The way they move—"

"If they see you first, you won't get that chance." He pulled me to the side. "Please, CJ. I can't do my job if I have to worry about you. Besides, the way the two of you are tromping through the woods, you'll scare away all the deer, and the hunters will move."

I leaned my head on his chest. "I'm no safer at home, but okay. We'll leave." It had been a stupid idea anyway. Sometimes, I needed my head examined for following Mags's ideas. I gave Eric a quick kiss, then headed back down the mountain leaving Mags to follow.

"Just our luck to run into Eric," Mags said.

"I have a tracker on my phone. I'm sure he saw it and came searching for me." I moved a low-hanging branch out of my face. "Which is why we have no choice but to do as he says. If we don't, he'll stop doing his job again to hunt us down."

"Stupid trackers." Mags stepped alongside of me. "There's no freedom anymore."

I cut her a sharp look. "We knew the general area because you put one on Larry."

She shrugged. "I didn't say I played fair."

I groaned and increased my speed, no longer caring how much noise I made. Noise meant not surprising a hunter or running into a deer that could be shielding us from someone with a gun.

"Wait a minute." I stopped and stared at a cut chain which once held our four-wheeler. Someone had cut through the lock.

"Larry is going to kill me." Mags heaved a sigh. "Is nothing safe anymore? Do you realize how long it will take us to walk back?" She started back up the mountain.

"Where are you going?" I jogged to catch up. My thighs didn't relish another climb.

"To find Larry. I'll have to admit to stealing his vehicle, throw myself on his mercy, and hope we can catch a ride back."

We hadn't gone far before two people, a man and a woman in camouflage sweats with scarves around their faces, blocked our path. Mags and I drew our guns, me knowing full well I couldn't do much damage with mine. "Nice gun straps," I said, making small talk. "Matching."

"Get my Taser," Mags whispered out of the side of her mouth.

"I can't or they'll shoot," I muttered back.

The man blinked rapidly. "Are you seriously whispering when we could shoot you at any moment?" The deepness of his voice alerted me to the fact he was disguising it.

"It does appear that way," I said. I'd once talked so much my captive couldn't wait to turn me over to someone else. That wouldn't work in this situation.

"Oh, my heart." Mags clutched her chest and dropped like a rock.

"Oh, hell." The woman muttered a bigger curse word and took off like a rocket into the thick brush.

"Woman, stay out of this," the man warned. "Take care of your friend, or the next time we'll shoot you both."

"Stay away from my dog." I knelt next to Mags. "They're gone. You can get up now."

The sound of an engine from a four-wheeler sounded from the direction the two had gone.

She opened her eyes. "How did you know I was faking?"

I rolled my eyes. "Because your cheeks are red, and your eyelashes kept fluttering. Let's go before they come back." I didn't really want to continue toward gunshots, so I took a seat on the ground and sent both Eric and Larry a text that said someone had stolen our ride and we'd be waiting for them when they finished.

It didn't take long for a return text and for my bottom to become numb on the cold ground. I glanced at my phone and grinned as I read the text from my uncle. "Did Mags take my extra four-wheeler?"

"I guess he knows me pretty well," she said, reading over my shoulder.

I responded yes and apologized for it having been stolen. Larry replied that we could sit and wait for a long time as punishment. I sighed and leaned against a tree.

"I wasn't sure what to expect, but it wasn't to see the two of you sleeping."

I opened my eyes to the sight of Eric with his side-by-side. "Mags got me up too early."

Eric smiled. "Larry asked me to fetch you. Since most of the hunters have gone, I'm here to give you a ride home."

My body felt frozen to the ground. "I think we'll need help up."

"I know I do." Mags groaned and rolled over to her hands and knees. "Be a gent and help us."

Laughing, Eric slid from his vehicle and helped Mags to her feet, then me. "Life sure isn't boring around you two. Come on. We'll call Davis when we get back and report the four-wheeler stolen."

On the trip home, I told Eric of us coming face-to-face with the very people we were looking for. "They're the ones who took the four-wheeler. I guarantee it."

That wasn't the only thing we had to report. We returned home to find Danny standing where my house used to be.

"Someone in a truck with deer antlers on the hood hooked up to your house and drove away."

Danny's eyes were huge. "I yelled for them to stop, but they kept on going."

I turned to Eric. "Caper is in the house. Those two poachers are really starting to make me mad."

Fifteen minutes after Eric called him, Davis arrived. The slam of his car door echoed in the winter morning.

"First thing, put down those guns." He scowled at us. "I will not take the chance of Mags pulling the trigger."

Eric took the guns from Mags and laid them carefully on the top of the picnic table. He slid his arm around my waist and pulled me close. "You're shivering."

"Cold and shock, I guess." He smelled of the outdoors—winter leaves and damp dirt over a subtle woodsy cologne.

Milton arrived soon after. Following him was Larry in his truck pulling my house.

I clapped my hands. "Where did you find it?"

"Down the road a couple of miles." He retrieved Caper from the backseat of his squad car. "This little thing is shook up but otherwise fine. Good thing I still had the keys to your house from when I had the unfortunate job of babysitting you."

"Good thing." I grinned and cuddled my dog under my chin. "Thank you. What I don't understand is why the two people who killed Robinson have caused me headaches but haven't tried to kill me."

"They ran me off the road," Eric pointed out. "That's an attempted murder in my book."

"Maybe they don't like to kill women?" Mags arched a brow. "I've heard some murderers have a conscience."

We moved to the side while Larry maneuvered my house into place. When he'd finished, he took a pole digger out of his truck bed and started digging a hole. "I'm going to cement a big ring into the ground so you can lock your house into place."

"Ingenious." Maybe we should do that with all the houses. I wasn't against new and improved safety measures. Despite the cold, I sat at the picnic table, reluctantly letting a squirming Caper down to do her business. "I'm not sold on the whole 'I don't kill women' thing. What if we're dealing with more than just the two in the deer truck?"

Davis sat across from me with Milton and Mags, leaving the spot next to me for Eric. "That's a good point, CJ. I'm starting to think the same. We've more than two people, and one of them is not afraid to kill."

Chapter Twelve

I took a nap that afternoon, curled up on the sofa with Eric. Snores let me know he still slumbered. Rather than get up and wake him, I lay still and pondered the morning and what, if anything, I'd learned.

Possibly more unsubs than in the deer truck. Check. A man and a woman…what if the two Mags and I had seen in the woods weren't the two in the truck?

I bolted upright. It's feasible they weren't the ones since they undoubtably took the four-wheeler. They would have been hard-pressed to make it back here to steal my house.

"What's going on in that head of yours?" Eric yawned and sat up.

I explained my thoughts. "I still believe the killers own the truck. But who are the two we met in the woods?" How could we draw out the two in the truck so the authorities could arrest them? So many questions. It seemed each day brought a tiny new clue that kept me digging until I was even more confused. I felt as if I was falling into a twenty-foot pit of lies and deceit.

Eric stared at me, a furrow forming between his brows.

"I'm trying to make sense of it all." I jumped to my feet and thundered up the stairs to retrieve the photos taken from Robinson's tent. I rejoined Eric and spread the pictures across the coffee table. "It was a dumb idea thinking Robinson stole the meat from the poachers. I think he *was* a poacher, and they got into a disagreement of some kind."

"I find it hard to believe my friend capable of such a thing." Eric's jaw set in a hard line. "You'll need to convince me."

"Look." I pointed to a photo that showed a bit of writing on a piece of tape holding the freezer paper together. "Ro for Robinson. This other tape shows ly, like it might be the last couple of letters." I squinted closer. "Might be a hy, a ke? Anyway, I think the poachers shared this cooler."

Eric crossed his arms and sat back. "Motive for Robinson to hunt out of season?"

I shrugged. "Is there a market for venison?"

"A big one, actually." His frown deepened. "I remember Robinson mentioning how tight money had been lately."

Bingo. "He was in partnership with the deer-truck people to sell venison as a way of making some fast money." Excitement leaped in me. "Now we have to find out why they killed him."

He groaned. "When I signed up to be a park ranger, I thought I'd patrol pretty campsites, check for licenses, and tell people to settle down when they became too noisy. I never had anything like this until I met you." He winked to take some of the sting out of his words.

There was truth in his words, and it caused a ping to my heart, but I laughed. "Lucky you. Now what?"

"I doubt the poachers stopped because Robinson is dead. Now that deer season is legal, the only way we'll catch them is if they kill more deer than tags, and that isn't even foolproof. They've already proven they're unscrupulous. They'll not bother with tags at all."

Eric stretched. "I'm going to see if I can't get some help from fellow rangers and up the surveillance of trucks leaving popular hunting areas. Maybe we'll get lucky."

Luck wouldn't have anything to do with whether or not they happened to stop the right truck. Persistence and a cool head were what always helped me catch the bad guys. That, and the bad guys coming to me, but I kind of wished they'd stop kidnapping me.

I cleaned up the photographs, put them back in a box in the bedroom loft and glanced out the window to see a car and truck parked outside of number four. It appeared the new owners of Amber's house had arrived. Time to meet them and introduce myself.

I told Eric where I was going and asked if he wanted to come along. He declined, saying he needed to go home and take care of some reports, exercise Hershey, and do laundry. "How about supper in two hours?"

"That sounds absolutely wonderful." I stretched up to kiss him. "There's some potato soup in the freezer. I'll heat it up."

"Yum."

Outside, Caper and I went one way while Eric went another. I waved at Mags, intending to drive past her house but found myself flagged down instead.

"Where are you going?"

"To meet the new people."

"That's where I thought you'd be going." She climbed into the cart, scooting Caper over. "I want to meet them."

I sighed. "I'll do the talking, okay? It isn't Amber's house anymore."

Her eyes widened in a pretense of innocence. "I'm just trying to be friendly."

"Right." The neighborhood spy didn't miss much, did she?

A curtain on the window fell into place as we stopped next to number four. When no one came out to greet us, I commanded Caper to stay and went to the front door. Since the porch was barely big enough for me to stand while the door opened, Mags had to stay on the steps. I rapped loudly and waited.

A man in his mid-thirties answered the door. "Yeah?"

I forced a smile despite his surly welcome. "Good afternoon. I'm the community manager, CJ Turley. I'm sorry I wasn't here to welcome you upon your arrival." Strange that I hadn't seen them arrive. I'd only napped for a couple of hours. "This is one of our residents, Mags Snyder."

"I'm Mike Langley. My wife's name is Dolly."

Mags waved. "Hello. My daughter used to own this house."

I rolled my eyes. "Is there anything you need to make your welcome more enjoyable?"

"Yeah, you can have those kids stop nosing around here." He jerked his head toward number six.

"The Flower children?" The oldest, Rose, had been in trouble before poking her little nose where it didn't belong, but she'd straightened up, I thought.

"I don't know their names. It's the little boys. They're always playing under our house."

"Briar and Sage?"

"I said I don't know their names. They scuttled out and took off running the minute we pulled up."

That hardly constituted always in my book, but I promised to speak to them. I couldn't help but glance at the hole in the grate around the house and wondered what in the world the boys could find interesting under there. A quick glance at the time on my phone showed I could catch the little rascals as they got off the school bus and drove the cart to the community entrance.

"Those children need more supervision," Mags said, crossing her arms. "Their mother is either gone or over at number three. Have you seen Dave Lincoln lately? Ripped."

"I'm assuming you mean fit." I watched the bus pull up. "No, I haven't had any need to speak to him." As a longtime resident who doesn't cause me trouble, I saw no need to bother the man. "The children are clean, fed, and have a roof over their head."

"I still can't fathom all those kids in a tiny house."

Neither could I but again not my business. "Hold up, boys," I said, stopping ten-year-old Briar and six-year-old Sage. "Hop on the back. I'll give you a ride."

"Are we in trouble?" Briar scowled.

"I don't know. Are you?" I arched a brow.

He shrugged and hopped on the back. Once both of them had a firm hold on the bar, I drove slowly to their house feeling a pang of guilt at the protest of their sisters. I didn't have room to give them all a ride.

I parked in front of their house and turned to face them. "May I ask what the two of you were doing under number four?"

"Burying a treasure," Sage said with a grin. He'd lost his two front teeth, I noticed.

"Really? What kind of treasure?"

"A secret one." Briar hopped down and grabbed his brother's arm. "Come on. We got homework."

"I don't." Sage yanked free.

"Liar." Rose came up behind the boys and ushered them toward the house. "You always have homework. Did you need something, CJ, Mags? I could use some extra money."

"I could pay you to dust," Mags offered.

Rose groaned. "You have too many knickknacks, but I'll be over in a bit. You'd better make it worth my time."

"Watch it or I'll change my mind."

I chuckled and turned the cart back toward my house. Ever since Rose was hired to help Mags after she'd broken her foot, the two seemed to enjoy spitting at each other like cats. At the house, I scooped Caper under one arm and invited Mags inside. "I've some ideas to run past you, and it's too cold to sit out here and chat."

"Oh, goody." Mags clapped her hands. "More news."

"You shouldn't be so excited." I unlocked the door and led the way inside. While she removed her coat and scarf, I filled her in on my assumptions.

She frowned. "That isn't news, CJ. That's speculation."

I curled my lip in a half smile. "I thought maybe you could give me some insight."

"Right." She snapped her fingers. "The diner in town serves venison burgers and steak this time of year. I say we go ask them where they get their meat."

My grin widened. "Sometimes your brilliance astounds me. We'll go there for lunch tomorrow. Any idea who the couple we met in the woods could be? My brain is tired."

She sat on one end of the sofa. "A girl can't think without tea."

I groaned and went to pop a pod into the coffee maker. "Earl Grey?"

"Yep."

Ann barged into the house, her cop mask in place. "You did what this morning?"

"Don't get so upset." Mags motioned for her to sit. "We went hunting."

"You stole Larry's four-wheeler, then it was stolen from you, and your house was stolen." She fell onto the sofa. "That's a lot even for you two."

"Tea?" I handed Mags her cup. "Where have you been?"

"On a goose chase that went nowhere. No thanks on the tea." Ann rested her head against the back of the sofa. "I went to the homeless community. Sometimes they know things we don't about people."

"We have a homeless community?" I frowned.

"Yep. A tiny house community like this one where people live free." She closed her eyes. "I guess they aren't technically homeless then, are they? Anyway, the same person who owns this land built another one about twenty miles from here. One man said he's seen the truck with deer antlers but didn't know who owns it. That's all I found out today."

"All day?" I sat across from her. "You left before we did, and Mags forced me out at an ungodly hour."

"I questioned every single person. Before that, I went to a friend's house to see if he could help me find a registration for the truck we're looking for. No luck there, since you don't have to register antlers."

"Cheer up." Mags patted her knee. "We're going to have venison for lunch tomorrow."

"Why?" Ann opened one eye.

"To find out who might be selling illegal meat."

Chapter Thirteen

I'd told Eric at supper about our plans to have lunch at the diner, but he couldn't make it. So, Ann, Mags and I slid into a red-vinyl booth and glanced at the laminated menus.

"I guess we have to order venison," Ann said, grimacing.

"Not necessarily." Mags peered at her over the top of the menu. "Just one of us does. Then, we marvel at how good it is and ask to speak to whoever does the buying. Or—" She held up a finger. "—we say we can offer a better deal on venison."

"Stick to the original plan. We don't have anything to sell." I shook my head. One day her ideas were wonderful; the next day they bordered on ridiculous.

Mags and I ordered venison burgers, leaving Ann to order a chef salad. "Not everyone can eat whatever and look like a teenager from behind," she said.

"I happen to have a good metabolism." I grinned and reached for the soda on the table in front of me. "My mother and grandmother were just as lucky. Don't be jealous. You're built perfectly fine."

"Then why aren't I in a relationship?" She tilted her head. "I'm thirty years old now."

"It's that face you make." Mags nodded.

"What face?" Ann frowned.

"That one where you look as if you have no feelings whatsoever."

"The cop face," I added. "It's intimidating."

"You two are ridiculous. It's part of my job. I don't wear that expression all the time."

"You do a lot." Mags grinned. "Whenever you want to look stern or you hear or see something you don't like or—"

"Fine. I get it. I'll try to do better."

"Do you go anywhere to meet a man?" I asked, straightening so the waitress could place our meals in front of us.

"Not really. Maybe I should do one of those online thingies."

I shuddered, having heard horrible things on a couple of the crime television shows I enjoyed. "Just wait. You'll meet someone." I bit into my burger. "This is good." I waved the waitress back over, wanting to get things moving. "Where do you buy your venison? It's delicious."

She scrunched up her face in thought. "Some guy brings it."

"Do you always have venison?"

"Most of the year. We like our meat fresh."

I met Ann's stern gaze. "Do you know who the

guy is? Does he drive a truck with antlers on the hood?"

"Yes, he does actually. Can I get you anything else?" She set the check on the table.

"His name?"

"You'd have to ask our chef. Want me to send him out?"

I nodded. "That would be great."

When she left, I grinned across the table at Ann. "That's how you get things done."

"You don't have all the info yet." She smiled back, motioning her head to where my newest neighbor from number four marched toward us.

"I didn't know you worked here, Mr. Langley." My smile widened, then faded at his scowl.

"I didn't know that moving to a small town meant everyone saw everyone on a daily basis. What do you want?"

I guessed being a chef didn't require people skills. "I'd like to know who you buy your venison from?"

"Why?" His face darkened.

"It's delicious. I'd like to buy some."

"You can buy it from me. I don't give out the name of my source."

A bit suspicious. "I can't imagine that your source wouldn't welcome another customer."

"He appreciates his privacy. Do you want some venison or not?"

"No, thanks." I slid from the booth and grabbed the check. "I wouldn't want to impose on any more of your time." Back straight, I headed for the register, leaving the other two to follow.

"That man is not a nice person," Mags said, sliding into the front passenger seat. "He doesn't deserve to own Amber's house."

"I'll do a search on him," Ann offered. "See what I can find out."

"Thanks." I glanced in the rearview mirror. While the man's attitude stung, I had to remember not everyone in town was nice. Most people liked me, so I shouldn't be bothered when the rare exception came around. "Where to now?"

"I'd like to see that other tiny house community," Mags said. "I wonder who's in charge there?"

"It's fine with me. Ann?"

"Sure." She typed something into her phone.

"Do you miss being a cop?" I asked.

"No. I like not having to follow such strict guidelines. Plus, I make more money." She flashed a grin, then returned to her phone.

"I kind of need directions."

"Oh, right. Head east."

I followed her instructions, merging with what little traffic there was in the middle of the day. "You'll have to glance up once in a while to tell me when to turn."

"Exit 108, then left. Go straight. You can't miss it."

I cut Mags an exasperated glance. "What are you doing back there, Ann?"

"Trying to find out something on Mike Langley." From her tone, all Ann let out was "duh."

I didn't seem to be having much luck with people being nice that afternoon. Ann's short but simple directions led us straight to the community named

Community. Not a very creative name. I pulled in front of house number one. A large sign on the door notified us this was where the manager resided. Should I have one on my house? I hoped not. It detracted from its cuteness.

"Y'all wait here." I opened the car door.

"I think not." Ann put a hand on my shoulder. "After the hunting escapade, you don't go anywhere without me.

I tisked loud enough for her to hear. "Fine. We'll all go knock on the door."

Turned out we didn't have to. By the time we reached the steps, a wiry, bearded man in a green golf cart pulled up alongside us.

"Can I help you?"

I thrust out my hand. "I'm CJ Turley, manager of Heavenly Acres. It's nice to meet you."

His amused gaze slid over me. "Hank Rivers. I wondered when you'd show up. I expected someone older and more manly."

He could have come and introduced himself to me just as well, but I kept that thought to myself. "I wasn't aware you existed, to be honest."

"We get that a lot. Want a tour?"

The place looked like a slightly messier version of Heavenly Acres, but I nodded. "I like the four-seater golf cart." I'd request one of my own as soon as I returned home. We piled into his cart, and soon we were zipping around the community like Mr. Toad's Wild Adventure Ride at Disneyland.

We made the tour in record time, skidding to a halt at number one. My cheeks were frozen, my toes were numb, and I think I lost a few years of my life.

"Uh, thank you. Everything looks…great."

"Now that we've got the preliminaries out of the way, what do you ladies really want? I've already spoken to the blonde today." He cocked his head.

I took a deep breath to steady my rattled nerves. "Have you remembered anything more about the truck with the antlers?"

"Nope. I've only seen it drive by the entrance. It's never actually come in here. Anyone with a truck like that has no need of free housing."

"What do you mean?" Hope sprang up. We might actually get a clue that meant something.

"I'm guessing you don't know your trucks. That particular Ford cost somebody at least fifty-thousand dollars. If they were homeless, they could sell it and buy a regular darn house."

Why would someone put antlers on such an expensive vehicle? "Where would someone hide something that expensive when they weren't driving it?"

"In a garage. Look, ladies, while it's nice to gaze upon such beauty, I've work to do." He turned the cart and sped off, leaving me with my mouth hung open.

"Doesn't he realize how many garages there are in Arkansas?" Mags scowled and marched to the car.

"I think maybe he means a rented garage," Ann suggested. "Still a lot of them, but not as bad as residential. I'll start calling around."

"Since Davis has an APB out on that truck, it's definitely hidden somewhere." I climbed into the driver's seat. Once Ann climbed in the back, we headed home.

Larry waited outside Mags's house. He sat on the folded-down tailgate with a deer next to him. "Anyone fancy some fresh meat?" He grinned. "Got me a good one but not good enough to win. That prize goes to Roy."

"My big hunter." Mags kissed him. "Skin that over at the campgrounds, not here."

"Roy won?" I grinned, happy for our handyman.

"Yep. Got him a ten-pointer and an increased bank account."

"You sound as if you had fun."

"I did. Learned a few things, too." His chest puffed. "I might tell you all about it over pizza."

"It's a deal. I'm buying." I hurried home to figure out how to fit everyone inside. While I loved all the seasons of Arkansas, there were times I wished the weather stayed nice all year. Having supper guests in autumn was one of them. No matter how I tried to move things around, there wasn't enough room. We'd have to eat outside. I'd ask one of the men to build a fire. Convinced we'd be cozy enough when the sun started to set, I placed a pizza order for delivery later that day. By the time I returned outside, Ann was on the phone and Larry and Mags were nowhere in sight.

Ann hung up the phone. "Davis said he'd get some men calling the places that rented space to vehicles. Let's hope they don't have the truck stashed in some barn."

Drat. I hadn't thought of that. Of course, I hadn't thought a couple of rednecks would own such an expensive vehicle only to mount part of a dead animal on the hood.

By the time Eric arrived, I'd convinced myself we'd never find the poachers. He told me to have faith and set about making a fire.

The pizza delivery arrived. Soon after, we gathered around the fire, plates balanced in our laps, and waited for Larry to tell us what he knew.

"I still don't have names," he said, "but we're definitely dealing with a man and a woman. Me and some of the other hunters started talking when we were tagging our kills. Seems we aren't the only ones upset about the poaching. It clears out too many of the animals for next year."

"This doesn't tell us anything." My shoulders slumped.

"Cheer up, sugar cup, we know for a fact we're dealing with a man and a woman. They've been seen, and I'm not talking about the two who stole my four-wheeler. I got that back, by the way." He shot Mags a glance. "It was left not too far from where we found you. Anyway, the two you spoke with are not our poachers. We're looking for two dark-haired people. Word around is that the ones who approached you are animal activists dead set against hunting of any kind, especially poaching."

"But they were armed and dressed for hunting." I set the pizza crust on my plate.

"Yep, but they weren't there to hunt for four-legged critters. Your new friends are wanting to stop the poaching as much as we do."

"Then why not let us know their identity?" I arched a brow.

"Because some people are smarter than you, sweetie." He grinned. "Anonymity makes it a lot easier not to have a target on your back."

I wrinkled my nose. "We need to lure our secret allies into the open."

Chapter Fourteen

The next morning, Eric worked too far away to take Hershey with him, since the dog was a handful for two good arms and Eric only had one. So, I strolled the community on an unusually mild morning with two dogs. I smiled and waved at everyone I passed and tried to ignore the silent Ann marching a few feet in front of me. My friend/bodyguard was as subtle as a wart on a nose.

A truck idled outside of number four. My unfriendly neighbor laughed and chatted with the driver. I wouldn't have thought the man had any smiles to share. He said something, chortled again, slapped the window frame and stepped back. When the truck turned around, I recognized Charlie from the youth center.

He smiled, Langley glowered, and I gave both of them the biggest grin I could and kept walking. It shouldn't have surprised me the two knew each other. In a small town, everyone knew everyone.

Ann strode toward the resident of number four. She introduced herself and handed him a business card. "I'm here on an unofficial capacity. CJ and I have been friends since we were young, but since you're new, I'd like to offer you my services."

I guess last year meant younger anyway. What was my friend playing?

The man looked a bit shocked. "Actually, I could use your services."

What? My eyes widened to where I most likely looked like an owl caught in the daylight.

"I think someone is following me—stalking me and my wife."

Ann motioned for me to join them and sat at the metal table erected in front of the house. "Please, sit and tell me why you think that."

He glanced at me.

"Don't worry about CJ. I often ask her to help me with some of the more mundane tasks," Ann said.

That part was backward, me being the one to enlist her help, but I went along with it. I looped the two dog leashes to the leg of the table and sat in one of the rickety plastic chairs. Out of the corner of my eye, I caught a glimpse of Mags working in a flower bed long since dead. Maybe I'd buy her a book on spying for Christmas. Her skills were sorely lacking in that area.

"My wife and I started feeling as if someone watched us right before hunting season began. We'd catch a glimpse of someone, sometimes two people, ducking out of sight when we turned around, always in the same place in the woods—those kind of things.

My gut tells me they have an unusual interest in us."

Ann pursed her lips. "Can you describe them?"

He shook his head. "A man and a woman, we think. That's it. They always keep their faces turned away or wear ski masks. Not unusual when the weather turns cold, but the masks are on every time we see them, which is at least once a day."

"Have you tried approaching them?" I asked. "Confronting the person often works for me."

He barely glanced my way. "They run off."

"We'll need to speak with Mrs. Langley at some point," Ann said.

"Does this mean you'll take our case?"

She nodded. "Send your email address to the one on my card, and I'll send you my fee." She stood and held out her hand. "I look forward to hearing from you."

Once we'd gone a couple of houses down, I said, "Spill it, girl."

"Yes, please." Mags jogged up next to us, then bent over and panted for breath. "I really need to hit the gym."

"Call it instinct," Ann said. "I can't figure out what it is about Mike Langley that bothers me."

"Other than the face he's rude and seems to dislike me?" I crossed my arms.

"Exactly. Everyone likes you unless they're doing something wrong and you've gotten involved." She turned and started walking again. "We can't attract too much attention. It could just be that the Langleys don't warm up to people easily."

"But it could be something else," Mags said. "Finally, we're getting somewhere."

Ann spun around. "Do not say anything about this to anyone. If the Langleys are suspect, we don't want to spook them."

"Is Larry still volunteering at the youth center?" I asked, pulling Hershey away from a half-eaten burger next to the garbage can. I picked up the litter and threw it away. Why couldn't people toss the trash into the can?

Mags shook her head. "Why?"

"Because the man Langley was talking to does." I grinned. "Guess I'll see if there's any volunteering I can do."

"Absolutely not." Ann frowned. "We'll ask Larry to see what he can find out from the other man."

"Yes, mom." I rolled my eyes but smiled. I knew how Ann would act toward my suggestions, but I made them anyway, just in case she surprised me. "Ask Larry to meet us for lunch." I aimed at Mags. "I don't want to waste any more time on this."

"The poaching has probably quit," she said.

"If there's money to be made, they won't quit. The diner said they serve venison year round."

"Which means they'll be hunting farther away from civilization," Ann said. "I gather nothing was discovered when tags were reported or the judging took place for the competition?"

"You would be right. Everyone abided by the law as far as Game and Fish could tell." I felt as if a vital clue hovered in front of me, but I was too blind to see it. I couldn't shake the idea it had to do with the meat in the cooler we'd found in Robinson's tent. "Where do you think Robinson's cooler is?"

"Evidence." Ann tilted her head. "Why?"

"I need to get to that meat."

"If you want more venison," Mags said, "go buy another burger." She frowned. "What's wrong with you?"

"Bear with me. What if there's a clue inside the meat? Eric has a hard time believing Robinson is as guilty as he seems. Maybe he is; maybe he isn't, or—" I held up a finger. "—he had a change of heart and hid something inside the meat."

Ann crossed her arms. "That's pretty far-fetched, even for you. Besides, we'd never reach the cooler without being arrested."

I was willing to take the chance. "Any rookies?"

"Yes." She narrowed her eyes. "I am not going to involve anyone new. But I will mention it to Davis."

My shoulders slumped. "You're a real party pooper, you know that?"

"I'm trying to keep you alive and out of jail. That's what you're paying me for."

We'd completed the circle and arrived back at my house. Mags said Larry replied to her text that he'd meet us for pizza at twelve-thirty. She rushed home to make herself pretty, leaving Ann and me to head inside my place.

"I didn't want to say anything in front of Mags," Ann said, sitting on the sofa and propping her feet on the coffee table, "but the friend I get help from sometimes might sneak us something from the cooler."

"Really? Can he be trusted?"

She stared at me as if I'd lost my mind. "I wouldn't be asking him for help if he wasn't trustworthy."

"Right. How soon can you get it done? How much can he get? How will he know which meat might contain a clue?"

"I'll have to trust his judgment." She typed into her phone. Seconds later, it rang, and she stepped onto the front porch to talk. When she returned, we left in her jeep to meet Larry, picking Mags up on our way.

A hostess seated us in a round booth and left us to decide what kind of pizza we wanted. We finally decided on a meat lover's with extra cheese.

Once the server left, Larry folded his arms on the table. "I'm not one to question an invitation from three beautiful women, but we aren't here for my charming conversation. You want something."

I gave my most beguiling smile. "We want you to volunteer again at the youth center and find out what you can about a friendship between Charlie and Mike Langley who lives in Amber's former tiny house."

"Please." Mags batted her eyelashes. "You're retired. What else are you going to do?"

"I'm retired so I can do exactly what I want when I want." He heaved a sigh when none of our smiles faded. "I'll see what they need me to do."

"You're the best uncle I've ever had," I said.

"I'm the only one you've had. A person would think you'd want to keep me around; not try and get me killed digging into stuff I have no business digging into." His sharp gaze landed on me. "Don't forget what keeps happening to you."

"I know." I'd faced death on more than one

occasion. Still, I didn't go looking for trouble. I simply stumbled across it.

Ann's phone vibrated on the table. She slid it close so I could read the screen.

Got a hunk. Bring it by later.

I did my best to keep my excitement from showing. There was no need for Mags to know anything about our further breaking of the law unless something came of it. She might be engrossed in the pizza the server placed in front of us, but Larry wasn't. He did the two-finger thing from his eyes to me, letting me know that he was watching me. I flashed another grin and toasted him with a slice of pizza.

After we ate, Larry headed to the youth center. Mags went along to see if she could help, which left Ann and me to head home alone. We spent a quiet afternoon reading and browsing the web until the sun set and a knock sounded at my door.

"I'll get it." Hand on the butt of the weapon hanging on her hip, Ann answered the door. "Hello, Brad."

A handsome man in his early thirties entered. While he acknowledged my existence, his blue eyes never left Ann's face. Someone seemed quite smitten with my bodyguard. Rather than complain about her lack of a relationship, why couldn't she see the possibilities right in front of her?

"I need to get this back ASAP," he said. "Can you look at it now?" He unwrapped a hunk of frozen deer meat and plopped it on my counter.

Ann pulled a butcher knife from a kitchen drawer and cut a slit in the meat. "Voilà. I love it when we get it right."

I peered around her. Nestled nice and snug in frozen venison was a separate wrapped bundle. Inside that bundle was a rolled-up wad of cash. It still didn't prove Robinson's innocence, but it did prove that my guess was right. It was about money, and Robinson was killed for it, but the poachers weren't smart enough to look in the cooler.

"I'd say this is a bit of cold, hard cash." I grinned. "Put this back, and I'll tell Davis to check the meat. Let him find it." I snapped a photo with my phone. Time to call the authorities. "How long until we're clear to call Detective Davis?"

"One hour." Brad cast one more longing glance at Ann and dashed out my front door.

Chapter Fifteen

By the next morning, Davis showed up on my doorstep. "I don't want to know how you knew or how a slice got cut in one of the chunks of meat, but we found over ten-thousand dollars. A man who owns a meat packaging plant says there's enough meat to come from three deer, maybe four."

I peered over the rim of my coffee cup. "That's awesome. Weird about the cut. Sad about all the dead deer."

"Right." He stepped into the house. "Where's Eric?"

"He sent a text that he'd be here around eight before heading to work. Why?"

"Reports of hunting where there shouldn't be. Got more of that coffee?"

I hurried to make him a cup. "You look tired."

"I am. We're getting nowhere finding Robinson's murderer. Milton is stretched thin helping two new recruits become familiar with this town." He plopped into a chair. "We need more cops. More detectives. More…something." He glared at Ann. "I need you back on the force."

"We're trying to help," Ann said. She sat across from him, her hands dangling between her knees. "What do you need from us other than me coming back? I like what I'm doing."

"Whatever info the two of you dig up. I'm not even going to try and tell you not to get involved. Right now, you're the best I've got."

Wow. If we were it, I felt bad for him. Yes, so far, I'd managed to keep myself alive and catch the bad guy, but I still wasn't trained for this type of work. It was more of a…twisted kind of hobby. "Why don't you ask Little Rock or Hot Springs for help?"

"With only one murder, not counting deer, it isn't important enough to call in the big guys. Their words, not mine."

"That's harsh." I frowned. "Robinson was our friend."

"That's not how I meant it. Tell Eric to call me—"

"I'm here." Eric cast me a smile. "Door wasn't locked, again." Hershey lumbered in, licking hands in greeting before taking his place under the coffee table.

"Davis and Ann are here." As if that made any difference.

"My fault." Davis rubbed his hands down his face. "Poachers again up past the waterfall. At least the department is getting calls to that effect."

Eric's expression turned grave. "I'll check it out today."

"Don't go alone." Davis shoved to his feet. "Those people have tried to kill you once already." Expression grave, he left, telling us to be careful, but if we were smart, we'd take a vacation somewhere far away.

I agreed with him about Eric being careful but not going on a vacation. Not until we found out what Robinson had been up to. Then, maybe Eric and I could go somewhere without stumbling across a murder. A girl could always hope. "Coffee before you head out?" I asked Eric.

"A thermos full, if you can imagine. It's unnaturally warm outside for this time of year, but I'm exhausted." He folded into a chair.

I ran my hand along his back on my way to the kitchen. "I'll make you a couple of sandwiches."

"You're a doll." He reached up and grabbed my hand before I got too far and pulled me down for a kiss.

I lingered for a moment, dispelling the niggle of fear at his heading back up the mountain alone. I cupped his face. "Come back to me."

A slow, sexy smile spread across his face. "Darlin' there's nowhere I'd rather be, but Parks and Rec needs my help."

I wanted to say that I needed him, but I knew my man's heart and held back the words. "I'll get that coffee." I pulled away and took the three steps to my kitchen. By the time I'd filled a thermos with coffee, made two ham and swiss sandwiches, and added a couple of store-bought chocolate chip cookies, Eric had fallen asleep.

"Aren't you going to wake him?" Ann glanced up from her laptop.

"Not yet. He's tired."

"The man has a job to do."

I wrinkled my nose at her and took a seat on the opposite end of the sofa. "The longer he's here, the longer he's safe."

An alert blared on all three of our phones.

Eric sprang to his feet.

I glanced out the window. A black, rotating spiral rope sped toward us. "Open the windows." I darted from one window to the next, shoving them up.

Caper and Hershey squeezed under the sofa.

The roaring of the tornado grew closer. We didn't have a storm shelter. Tiny houses weren't built for winds of this magnitude. We'd never had a twister in the area before.

I swallowed past the lump in my throat as the wind lashed at my hair and blew things off my shelves. "I don't know what to do."

"We get out of here." Eric whistled for the dogs and took my hand, leading me outside. He glanced in all directions. "The iron picnic tables are bolted to the ground, right?"

I nodded. "Will they be enough?"

"It's better than what we have now."

With the increasing wind buffeting us, we ran to the playground area and crowded under a table. The Flower family had the same idea and Lucy cowered under one with all six of her children linked together by a rope. Other residents either sped toward the highway in their cars or stared wide-eyed at the approaching twister.

I screamed for them to find shelter, only to have my words ripped away on the wind. Leaves and twigs struck my uncovered arms, leaving tiny cuts. We'd never survive a direct hit.

A tree snapped in half, falling between houses four and six. My house and number five were pushed over. Then, as if God had reached down and plucked it away, the twister dissipated before hitting us. I prayed no one had been killed or injured.

I crawled from under the table and stared across the lake. They'd have fared better being a bit further from the actual twister. Still, tents ripped from their stakes lay flattened and sodden at the water's edge.

"I need to check on everyone." I turned to Ann and Eric. "I have a group text I send. I'll need your help to locate those who don't show up. Ann, please check to see if Mags is home." Not seeing Larry's truck gave me hope she wasn't in the tipped-over house.

"I'm not going anywhere today." Eric patted my shoulder.

I pulled my phone from my pocket and sent the group text, asking everyone to come immediately to the common area for roll call. Slowly the residents exited their homes. It was a quiet group that gathered around me.

"No one in Mags's place," Ann said, returning to the group. "I'm sure she and Larry were at the youth center."

A woman I didn't recognize came out of number four. It had to be the elusive Mrs. Langley. She glanced around, faltered at the sight of a tree limb through the window of her car, then ambled toward us and stood on the outside fringes of the group.

"I've called for help picking up the overturned houses," Eric said.

"We're here!" Mags waved out the window of Larry's truck as they pulled up next to us. "My house is lying on its side."

"So is mine." I took a deep breath and glanced around the people I was responsible for. "We're lucky. Everyone is accounted for and damage minimal."

"No." Mags shook her head and pointed at her house. "My things will be shattered."

"Possessions can be replaced." I'd have some broken things of my own, but we and our dogs were safe. "Has anyone heard how bad the damage in town is?"

"Yes." Larry set his jaw. "F3 took out some houses, damaged the diner, and one man is missing. This tiny house community was lucky."

"Not just lucky," I said. "Someone above looked out for us. Anyone available to help clean up?"

Most hands raised except for Mrs. Langley who sneered and returned home. She took a two-handed grip on the tree limb and pulled it from her car window. Not any more friendly than her husband.

Shrugging, I turned back to the others, please to see Roy already at work cleaning up fallen tree limbs and scattered garbage. Eric secured the dogs to Caper's lead line next to my house and went to wait for the men who'd right our houses. Other than scattered shingles, blown-away lawn furniture and ornaments, nothing was damaged that couldn't be replaced.

I motioned for Ann to follow and made my way to Mrs. Langley's house. "Sorry about your car. I hope you have insurance."

"Of course, I do."

I glanced at the open door to her house, shocked to see several deer heads mounted on what little walls she had. One large buck head would have taken up a lot of room, but three? "You and your husband enjoy hunting."

"Who doesn't around here?" She crossed her arms. "Is there something I can help you with?"

"No, I came to offer my services." I smiled.

She jerked her chin toward my house. "Looks like you need it more." She turned and marched into the house, slamming the door.

I couldn't help but hope it would rain soon and her roof would leak because of several missing shingles. "Let's go see what we can do about some of my things."

"What was that all about?"

"I wanted a look inside. If she were renting, I'd just have to give notice. As a homeowner, I can't go inside unless invited. Lots of deer stuff."

"Hmmm. They bear watching, although I can't find anything bad about them online or in the police records."

"Maybe Larry's had some luck." I'd ask him after things settled down for the day.

An hour later a crane stood my house upright. I squared my shoulders and stepped inside. Overturned furniture, shattered glass, and whatever hadn't been inside cupboards lay scattered everywhere.

From the loft, I could see the bookshelf I used as a wall divider still remained in place. The screws I'd used to bolt it to the floor had held. Despite a few broken windows, the house was still livable. I blinked back tears and got to work, Ann at my side helping.

A few seconds later, I chuckled. "As many times as I've had someone try to kill me, this is the first time I've almost gotten blown away by a force of nature."

"That isn't funny," Eric said from behind me. "Anytime I almost lose you is one time too many."

I rushed into his arms and gazed into his face. "I'm always safe as long as you're with me."

"The problem is I can't always be with you. When I'm not, you get into trouble."

"That's why Ann is here." I smiled. "Ann, go outside."

"Okay." She frowned and slipped past us.

"I want a kiss, Eric Drake. One to make me blush." One to remind me I still lived and loved. "I love you."

He whispered, "I love you," against my lips, then gave me a kiss that curled my toes.

Someone cleared their throat from my open door.

I pulled reluctantly away from Eric to see Larry looking amused. "What?"

"Do you want to know what I learned today or not?" He wiggled his eyebrows. "Because I might have found your activist."

Chapter Sixteen

"Who?" I held my breath, anxious yet nervous to hear his answer.

"Charles Campbell." He grinned.

"The Charlie from the youth center?" My eyes widened. "How do you know?"

"Well, I've heard him complaining into his phone that they weren't doing enough to stop the poaching."

I perched on the arm of my easy chair. "You think 'they' means Charlie and someone else?"

Larry nodded. "Yes, but I'll keep my eyes and ears open to learn more. Just wanted to tell you your hunch might be right. There's a lot to learn doing volunteer work." He flashed a wink and left us alone.

Not exactly good enough to warrant breaking up a steamy kiss from Eric, but it was a possible step forward. "We need to find out for sure." I met Eric's gaze. "Then if Charlie is the activist, we can team up together."

Eric sighed. "I'll just ask the guy. I'm pretty good at knowing if someone is lying."

"Too bad we don't have a poacher suspect standing in front of us," I said with a grin and resumed putting my house to rights. Eric went outside to volunteer whatever help a one-armed man could give before going to the dealership to pick up his new ride.

Ann reentered and taped cardboard over one of the shattered windows. "I think Eric outright asking Charlie could be a good thing."

"But?" I tilted my head.

"If Charlie is the poacher, it could be bad."

"Good point." Why couldn't we get a break that didn't come with a warning label?

By the time my house was as good as I could get it and Ann had carried what couldn't be salvaged to the dumpster, the rest of the community appeared to be put back together. Larry, bless his heart, had ordered enough pizzas for everyone and the mood in the common area was joyful, despite the lowering evening temperatures and the day's earlier fear.

I glanced at number four. Mr. Langley had returned home and every light was on. Someone had taped plastic over his car's windshield.

"Do you think they'd come if we invited them in person?" Ann took a bite of a slice of pepperoni pizza. "I could go over on the pretense of asking whether they received my fee chart."

"Great idea." This time, I elected to stay with the group rather than endure more scathing glances from either of the Langleys.

Rose Flower and Danny Olson rocked back and forth on the swings, both looking rather melancholy. I ambled their way and sat in the last swing. "Why the long faces?"

"Mom wants to marry Mr. Lincoln." Rose swiped away her tears. "That means we have to move. I like it here."

"Moving would mean a bigger house." I gave her a reassuring smile.

"My friends are here." She glanced at Danny from under lowered lashes.

I always made it a point to try and help my residents, but this was a problem I couldn't solve. I'd hate to see the Flowers go and hoped they'd find a way to stay when they became Lincolns, but their house already burst at the seams with growing children.

Glancing toward number three, I wasn't surprised to see Lucy leaving Dave's house. Now would be a good time to offer my congratulations. "I'm glad to see you two survived the tornado." I stopped at the bottom of the steps.

"Except for a few broken dishes, everything is fine." Dave leaned on the railing. "You? Saw your house turned over."

"Nothing that can't be fixed. Rose told me the good news."

Lucy paled. "What good news?"

"That y'all are getting married. She's bummed that you'll have to move—"

Lucy frowned and glanced at Dave. "We aren't getting married."

A flicker of worry crossed his face. "Kids get the

craziest ideas."

Something felt off about the whole conversation. Rose might be a teenage girl, but she seemed mature for her age and not the type to get worked up over something she wasn't sure of. "Where do you think she got that idea?" I glanced from Lucy to Dave and back to Lucy.

Lucy shook her head in nervous jerks. "I have no idea. See you bright and early in the morning, Dave." She squeezed past me. "Good night, CJ."

"Good night." I watched her leave before turning to Dave. The man met my gaze. While I knew him as a resident, something about him seemed familiar. As if I'd spent time with him outside of the community. Ridiculous. I shrugged and headed back toward my house. I passed Dave's truck and glanced at the gun rack in the window. Two rifles with matching gun straps of camouflage green hung there. I whirled.

Dave stared after me, his face stony. I wanted to mention my suspicions but kept my mouth shut. Activist or poacher? I gave him a thin-lipped smile and a short wave before returning to the common area.

Spotting Lucy and Rose off to the side, I skirted the area and used a tree for cover.

"Where did you get such a crazy idea?" Lucy hissed. "I don't ever plan on getting married again."

"I heard you and Dave talking about moving and being partners."

"That doesn't mean what you thought. Ugh. You're going to ruin everything."

"Mom, I don't know what you're talking about."

I peered around the tree. Lucy paced, her hands

in fists at her sides.

"We're trying to do something good here, Rose. Please don't assume anything. If it's a matter that concerns you, I'll tell you."

"What are you doing?" Someone tapped me on the shoulder.

I shrieked and clamped a hand over my mouth, staring with wide eyes at a grinning Mags. I gave a vigorous shake of my head.

Mags didn't pick up on my not-so-subtle hint. "Hello, Lucy, Rose." Mags stepped out from behind the tree. "Sorry if I scared you. I saw a mouse."

"How long were you there?" Lucy asked.

"I just walked up. Why? Do y'all want pizza? There's plenty left."

Bless my dear friend, Mags. She knew the right time to create a diversion.

I made a wide circle back to the common area. Ann had just returned from the Langleys. I pulled her aside. "Well?"

"They aren't interested in getting to know their neighbors, and my fees are too high." She gave a sly smile. "I set foot inside their house, though. Talk about a hunter's tiny paradise. Everything's camouflage this and camouflage that."

"Are they our poachers?"

She shrugged. "Who knows? A lot of people in this state like camouflage. Where were you?"

"Eavesdropping." I filled her in on my conversations with Dave and Lucy, then the one between Lucy and her daughter. "Their guns match the ones of the thieves who stole the four-wheeler."

She raised her eyebrows. "Camouflage?"

"Right. Got it." My shoulders slumped. Still, I was onto something. I knew it. "They warrant watching, Ann. My gut tells me not to shove them aside." We had three pairs of suspects for the activists—Charlie and a woman, Dave and Lucy, and the Langleys. One pair could also be our poachers. Of course, the poachers could be people I hadn't met yet. How did one draw a poacher into the open?

By the time the impromptu survival party broke up, I wasn't any closer to formulating a plan. I heaved a heavy sigh and trudged home.

"What's wrong?" Mags bustled next to me. "You're thinking so hard, flames are coming out the top of your head."

"Come inside and I'll fill you in. Ann thinks I'm overthinking things."

"You?" She made a mock face. "Not a chance."

"Very funny." I glanced over to where Eric spoke to Larry through the window of Larry's truck. "Have you noticed how many people drive trucks?"

"Yep. Makes me feel left out sometimes."

I untied the two dogs from the line and let them scamper into the house. Once inside, I locked the door and told her the same things I'd told Ann.

"So, that's why you were sneaking around behind the tree." She grinned. "Good work. I agree with you."

"Of course, you do." Ann opened her laptop. "Plan all you want. I'm still trying to find a storage place for the antler truck."

"There can't be that many places around here." I glanced around my house. Already minimalist in content, the place looked really bare, absent the broken things. A trip to a discount store was in my future. I wanted the house to look lived in despite its small size. "Storage units, anyway. What about checking old buildings and barns?"

"Why hasn't Davis put a description of the truck on the news?" Mags asked. "I guarantee you someone will have seen that truck."

"He doesn't want to tip off the owners. I'll talk to him again. We definitely need help from the public."

Exhaustion immediately settled on my shoulders like a weighted blanket. Not the kind that's supposed to be comforting, either. This one made it hard to breathe. The adrenaline that had kept me going all day poured out as if I were a bucket full of holes. I sat, leaned my head back and closed my eyes, half listening to Ann and Mags bicker about what our next step should be. I wanted to focus on finding the activists, engaging their help, and seeking the answer to the ever-elusive question of why Robinson was involved and murdered.

I opened my eyes to the sight of an orange glow in the sky coming through my window. I struggled to my feet and stared outside. Across the lake, a fire raged where Robinson's trailer stood.

"Fire!" Eric dashed past the window.

Chapter Seventeen

I locked the dogs in the house and sprinted for my golf cart, Mags and Ann on my heels. If someone set fire to Robinson's trailer, then I'd missed something vital when I'd searched the place.

By the time we reached the trailer, it and the storage shed were nothing more than smoldering hunks of metal and wood. I wrapped my arm around Eric's waist and leaned into him, the heat from the fire warming my face. "Accident or arson?"

He shrugged. "The department will figure it out."

I peered into his face. "Are you okay?"

With a sigh, he gave me a sad smile. "I'd really hoped Robinson was nothing more than someone in the wrong place at the wrong time. It's hard to think a friend could be messed up in something like this."

"We might still prove him innocent." My heart broke at his sadness. It wasn't like Eric to be so down.

"Looking less and less likely." He turned away and headed to the fire truck that had pulled up.

"Poor thing." Mags glanced his way. "We need to speed things up and get that man feeling normal."

"I don't know how." If only we could find that darn truck with the antlers. Then, we could wipe the mud off the license plate and find out who owned the vehicle. "Other than drive the backroads and hope we get lucky."

"Great idea. We'll go tomorrow. I'll borrow Larry's truck."

I narrowed my eyes. "Don't steal it."

"Beg, borrow, steal—what's the difference?" She flashed a grin. "Just don't tell him why."

"You've turned into a delinquent, Mags." I shook my head and joined Eric and the fire chief.

"See the stain on the concrete slab?" The chief pointed to a charred section. "Looks like an accelerant."

Arson. I knew it. What had been here that someone needed to destroy the place?

"I don't like Mags's idea of wandering the countryside aimlessly," Ann said, her voice low.

"Do you have a better idea?" I wasn't keen on it either but would try anything.

"I'm trying. At least let me print out a Google Map of the area so we can formulate some kind of plan."

"Okay. We leave first thing in the morning."

"Where are we going?"

I spun around and gazed into Eric's face. "Crazy, want to go?"

"Sweetheart, you're already there. What are you

three women cooking up?" The stormy look on his face left no room for skirting the issue.

"We're going to search for the deer truck tomorrow."

His gaze hardened. "Okay. I'll clear my schedule."

I blinked a few times. "You're going with us?"

"Oh, yeah. No way I'm letting you out in these woods without me. I know this mountain; you don't."

Relief flooded through me. Having Eric with us would be wonderful. I trusted his instincts way more than I did Mags's or even Ann's. "I'm so glad."

"I'm not happy about it, CJ, but I want this over." He marched to his side-by-side. "See you back at the house."

"I don't know this Eric," Ann said.

"Neither do I." But then again, the past mysteries we'd been involved in weren't because of the death of a close friend.

Davis waited at the house, clearly not happy. "The chief told me it's probably arson."

"Did you just come from Amber's?" I nodded at his mussed hair.

"Yeah, she's having me try on tuxes she had delivered." A smile played at his lips. "I was kind of happy to have an excuse to stop."

"Let's go inside. It's freezing," I suggested.

"I'm going home. See you in the morning." Mags put a finger to her lips as she passed behind Davis.

He gave her a stern look over his shoulder. "I don't want to know what that's about."

I grinned. "Wise choice." I unlocked the front door, let the dogs out, since Caper minded better when the well-trained Hershey was around, and ushered everyone in. "Coffee?"

"Why does everyone always offer coffee when they get together?" Ann raised her brows. "Have you noticed that? I'd rather have water."

"Okay." I shot a quick glance at the ceiling. Had everyone around me been changed into people I no longer knew? Aliens?

"I'll take coffee," Eric said. "It'll warm me up."

"Make that two." Davis sat next to Eric on the sofa, and the two spoke in whispers. A few seconds later, Ann sat on the coffee table and joined their huddle.

Fine. If it weren't so cold outside, they'd have hunkered down at the picnic table to talk where I couldn't hear. Trouble for them was…I had excellent hearing. I made myself busy so I didn't look suspicious.

"We've managed to eliminate any storage buildings or barns in this area." From the corner of my eye, I could see Davis spreading a paper between him and Eric. A map of the mountain was my guess.

"We thought to search this area tomorrow," he said. "If you could go here—"

"I'll have the women with me."

"No way."

"They won't be deterred," Eric said. "I don't blame them, anyway. We're safer together."

"You can all be eliminated at once, you mean."

"We'll cover more ground by splitting up," Ann said. "If Eric doesn't allow CJ and Mags to go along, they'll go anyway. I can't protect them both by myself."

"This is the most hardheaded group of people I've had the misfortune to know." Davis scowled.

"Still want your coffee?" I smiled and held out a cup.

"No." He stormed outside, then poked his head back in. "It's raining. Might want to let the dogs in." Then back out again.

"I'll do it." Ann stepped outside, shouted, and the sound of footsteps thundered down the steps.

Eric and I raced outside to see her and Davis leap into his car and speed off. "What did we miss?" I took a sip of coffee from the cup I'd made Davis and glanced at Eric.

"My guess is they spotted the truck." He held his mug to his lips.

"Maybe they'll catch them."

"Nope. I saw a screwdriver poking out of Davis's tire."

Sure enough, they stopped before passing through the front entrance. Davis jumped out, took one look at his tire, and kicked it. He moved to the other side and kicked that flat tire too.

Eric handed me his cup and leaned over to give me a kiss. "Guess I need to give him a ride. Stay safe inside tonight, CJ."

"Guaranteed." I called the dogs out from under the house and let them in.

Ann marched through the drizzle toward me while Eric headed to Davis. Things were never boring at Heavenly Acres or Blue Lake Campgrounds.

"I guess you heard everything," Ann said, letting me enter the house first.

"Yep. Anything interesting about the area we'll be searching?" I set Eric's cup in the sink, then joined Ann on the sofa to finish mine.

"Not really. Less populated than where Davis will be searching, which might be good for us. Fewer barns to peek into."

"What about a chicken house?"

Her brow furrowed. "What?"

"We didn't think about chicken houses. They're plenty big enough to hide a truck inside."

She smoothed out the map Davis had left behind. "There are several chicken farms where we'll be searching. How in the world will we get inside?"

I shrugged. "We'll pretend to be buying eggs?"

"That doesn't mean they'll let us in the house."

True. "Mags is great at causing a distraction." I grinned.

"That she is." Ann raised her hand for a high-five.

"Next question." I gave her the hand slap. "What was that deer truck doing here right after someone burned down Robinson's trailer?"

"To burn down the community," we said in unison.

I mentally apologized to Eric. "I have a responsibility to make sure nothing is happening out there."

"I know." Ann shrugged into her jacket.

I grabbed mine from a hook next to the door. "We'll have to walk. I'd like to take the dogs. They'll alert us if anyone is around."

"Good idea. I'll take Hershey. Caper doesn't mind me."

Caper didn't mind anyone most of the time. I handed Ann a leash, then locked the door behind us.

Please, God, don't let anyone burn down my house.

I glanced overhead at one of the security cameras so my photo would be taken. I'd do the same at each one as we passed so if something happened to me, Eric and Davis would have a time stamp of each place.

It was hard to sniff for smoke even in a light drizzle, but I kept trying anyway. Caper pranced alongside me as if we were on a Sunday stroll through a park. Hershey kept stopping to lift his leg on everything. It wasn't until he froze mid-leg that the hair on my arms also lifted.

"Ann," I hissed, motioning to the dog.

Hershey stared toward number four. He growled deep in his throat, then gave a sharp bark.

I yanked him behind house number two and put my hand around his muzzle. "Do we go looking?"

Ann nodded. "But you stay behind me."

The window above my head opened. Mark Boyles grinned down at us. "What are you two doing?"

"Shh."

"Oh, I see. CJ is snooping again."

"Seriously, Mark. Hush or I'll have Ann shoot you."

He held up his hands in a mock salute. "Stepping away."

Grinning Baboon ruined our cover. Hershey sat at Ann's feet and stared up at her.

"Whoever it was is gone." She glared toward the

now-closed window. "Let's keep going."

I doubted it would do any good, but we kept walking. A faint glow illuminated the wet night as we neared the curve of the road. Flames licked the top of a trash can.

I banged on the door of number fourteen. "I need your fire extinguisher."

The elderly man who lived there shuffled past me and aimed at the fire. "I got this."

"Did you see anyone?" Ann asked after the fire was out.

"Nope. Probably kids playing games." He hunched his shoulders against the chilly rain and shuffled into his house.

"Let's go home," I said. "I'm cold. Why would the arsonists who burned Robinson's trailer stoop to something as small as a trashcan?" My eyes widened. "A distraction."

I sprinted home. My heart sank at the sight of my front door hanging open, the frame around the handle splintered. I took two steps at a time.

The coffee table lay empty. "The map and your laptop are gone."

"No." Ann clenched her fists. "At least it's password protected, but all my notes are on there." She yanked her phone from her pocket and punched some buttons. "Bring Davis back. Someone broke in."

They must have been on their way back, because they barged through my ruined door in less than five minutes. I explained about how someone lured us outside, then occupied us with the trash-can fire.

"Whoever it is lives close," I said. "They're

watching me. They know how I'll react to any given situation." Which totally creeped me out.

"You can't stay here tonight," Eric said. "You shouldn't stay anywhere near here."

"I'll take her to her grandmother's house," Ann said. "Come pick us up bright and early in the morning. Someone will need to bring Mags. We'll also need another copy of that map. Are we all agreed we won't let this stop us?"

Three heads nodded.

Davis didn't look pleased that Ann had taken control of the situation, but he didn't argue. "Good luck tomorrow. Be safe. Keep your phones on at all times. Check in regularly."

"You do realize cell service sucks on the mountain, right?" A muscle ticked in Eric's jaw. "We can't rely on backup."

Chapter Eighteen

It was a grim but determined foursome that climbed into Eric's jeep he'd purchased the day before. He ran his hand over the dashboard. "I hope she doesn't get wrecked. I'd like to keep her for more than a day."

"With four pairs of eyes looking in all directions, we should have advanced notice of anyone coming after us." I patted his arm.

"Sure." Mags leaned her elbows on the back of the seat. "We'll protect your new baby."

Eric sighed. "Seatbelts." He punched a coordinate into a dashboard GPS and headed to where we hoped to find answers to all our questions.

"Too bad we don't have an article of clothing from the poachers," Mags said. "Then Hershey could track them and save us a lot of time."

"He wouldn't be able to track them inside a truck going down the Interstate." Eric glanced in the

147

rearview mirror.

"Just tossing out ideas since Ann's no help. She's asleep."

"No, I'm not. There isn't anything to do until we reach the area so I might as well rest. Things might get ugly in a few hours."

"Thanks for that particular reminder." I slumped in my seat and leaned my head against the window, following Ann's advice. I must have fallen asleep, because the crunch of new tires on rocks woke me. I sat up and swiped the hair out of my face. "We're here."

"Only to the first building on the map." Eric parked at the end of the driveway. "We walk from here. I don't want to take any chances with my jeep."

Ann groaned and shoved open her door. "Good thing I wore hiking boots. Bundle up, folks. It's cold."

I cracked open my window so the dogs could have some air, then followed the others up the gravel drive to where three chicken houses sat. This early in the morning, everything was quiet except for Caper's yipping from the jeep.

"Do we start looking in windows?" I glanced at Eric. "I don't want to get shot for trespassing."

"I didn't see any signs. We won't go in the buildings, just look."

We split up, Mags going with Ann and me following Eric. Fifteen minutes later, we saw no sign of any vehicle except a John Deere tractor and a rusty pickup.

"Can I help you?" An older man with a gray beard and wearing a red and black flannel jacket approached us.

"I'm Park Ranger Eric Drake. We were told the owner of a Ford truck with antlers mounted to the hood lives here."

"Well, Mr. Park Ranger, you were told wrong. That old rust bucket you see is the only truck I own, but I've seen the one you're talking about." He tilted his head. "They done something wrong?"

"I'm not at liberty to say." Eric smiled. "They've headed up the mountain?"

"On occasion." He crossed his arms. "Are these women rangers, too?"

"They're just along for the ride. Thank you for your time, Mr.—"

"Jacobs. Harvey Jacobs and this here is Jacobs Chicken Farm. If you find my no-good son, John, tell him to get his butt home. He's been gone a few days, and I need his help." With those dismissive words, the man trudged away.

Eric chuckled. "Looks like we're headed up the mountain."

"I wouldn't laugh if I were you," Mags said. "I've heard folks aren't friendly the higher you go."

"Don't believe everything you hear," Eric said. "Just do what I say, and you'll be fine."

She gave a jaunty salute and climbed back in the jeep.

A few minutes later, Eric pulled the jeep in front of a path where tire tracks led away from the road. He turned off the ignition. "Let's go. Bring the dogs. I don't know how far we'll have to walk."

I hurried to the back of the jeep, grabbing the leashes the second the back was open so the dogs

149

couldn't dash away. I handed Hershey's leash to Eric and kept a firm grip on Caper's. The last thing I wanted was for her to run off into the thick underbrush. Everything prickly liked to tangle in her fur.

"No cell service," Ann announced holding her phone high. "I thought we'd have service longer. I hope we aren't being lured like four big bass."

"Large or small mouthed?" Mags wiggled her eyebrows.

Ann glanced at her. "Definitely large mouthed." Ann grinned and stepped back to take the rear.

"Let's keep the noise down," Eric said. "No sense announcing our arrival to anyone that might be unfriendly."

I agreed. It wouldn't be hard to hide in the bushes and take a shot at one of us. That idea had me whipping my head back and forth until I feared it might fly off.

Eric took my hand. "Relax, sweetheart. I'm here."

"At least it's daylight. I'm not a fan of the woods at night." Too much running for my life in the dark. But Eric was right. This time I wasn't alone.

The path took us to a dilapidated barn full of woodpecker holes and weathered to a smoky gray. Wood of this type was a designer's dream.

"It's gorgeous." Or it used to be. It was also easy to see the barn held nothing but rusty wood tools and weeds. A wasted trek through the woods.

"On to the next," Mags pointed at the sky and turned back to where we'd left the jeep. "I wonder how Davis is faring. We won't know when, or if, we can go home."

"We'll update each other every chance we can. There will be pockets of service up here around homes, maybe." Eric shrugged.

"What homes?" I heaved a sigh. "I'm cold and tired."

"Let's break for lunch once we get to the jeep." He squeezed my hand. "I wish I had a better plan than us manually searching for the truck. At least it's been spotted up here."

I smiled. "We could look at this as a date. A hiking, sightseeing, treasure-hunting sort of date."

"With two chaperones." He leaned down and gave me a quick kiss.

Sandwiches and thermoses of soup waited for us back at the jeep. Eric started the engine and let the heater warm us while we ate.

"You ladies can stay in the vehicle while I search the next stop, if you'd like." He took a bite of his ham and swiss.

"No, that would have you out there alone. We're all in this together, success or failure." If we did find the truck, Eric had been instructed to one…send Davis the GPS coordinates, and two…place a tracker somewhere it wouldn't be easily detected. The whole idea left too many possibilities of discovery in my opinion. Maybe Milton should have come with us. We weren't law enforcement. Sometimes Davis's relinquishing of total control and requesting my help were asking a little too much. I'd gone from "nosy and meddling" to "you should join the police force."

Far too soon Eric announced break was over and drove us farther up the mountain. The sun broke through the clouds promising a little respite from the cold.

When we stopped this time, I shrugged out of my top layer and glanced around. "I don't see a road." I frowned.

"Tire tracks." Eric knelt next to bent weeds. "Fresh, too. See how they're broken?"

"Sure." Not really. I'd seen tracks in green grass, but dried weeds were too much for my meager tracking skills.

Ann pulled her weapon from her hip holster. "It's thick in there. I'm going to expect the worse." Her cop face fell into place.

Eric pulled his gun, too.

Mags clutched her Taser.

Eric narrowed his eyes. "If you zap me, I'll shoot you."

"Sometimes, you carry a grudge far too long." She rolled her eyes. "Both times I zapped you were accidents."

His face darkened. "I'm not completely convinced." He stepped in front as we formed a line—him, me, Mags, and last Ann.

Everyone had a weapon but me. All I had was a small dog who acted as if we were on a pleasure excursion. She pranced alongside me, a look of rapture on her furry face. I could always tell her to attack the bad guy's ankles. I grinned at the cutie, then my gaze locked on Eric's strong back.

And I promptly tripped over a tree root, landing face first in a pile of decaying leaves. Ugh. They smelled like rotting meat.

"Are you okay?" Eric helped me up and wiped

leaves and dirt from my face.

I nodded. "I wasn't watching where I put my feet."

"If you were watching," Mags said, "you might have noticed what you fell into."

I glanced down to see a bloated face of a man who'd been there for days. My eyes widened, and I rubbed the sleeve of my flannel shirt over and over my face to dispel the remains of the dead man on my cheeks.

"Anyone have phone service?" Eric held his high.

"Nope." The other two checked their phones. I was too busy trying not to lose my ham and cheese.

"Who do you think he is? One of the poachers?" I leaned one hand against a nearby tree trunk and took deep breaths.

"No way of knowing," Eric answered. "He might not be related at all. He might have trespassed." He nodded toward a no-trespassing sign.

"Then why would someone leave him on this side of the fence and bother burying him under leaves?" Ann stared down at the body. Taking a deep breath and holding it, she swept aside the leaves and searched his pockets. "Oh, he's ripe." She located a wallet and looked at the driver's license. "Looks like we found John Jacobs."

"Do we head back and let his father know or keep looking for the truck?" I straightened, keeping my gaze averted from the body.

"I think we should let his father know," Ann said, "but not bring the man up here. This might be a crime scene."

"I agree." Eric kicked leaves back over John Jacobs. "Let's head back down. We can always search the rest of the mountain tomorrow."

The four of us made our somber way back to the jeep.

Eric stuck an orange cone between the branches of a tree so we could find the spot again. "Ann, send Davis a text. He'll get it whenever we pass out of the dead zone."

I didn't recall any missing persons on the evening news this week, but then I didn't have a lot of time to watch television. Something I intended to remedy as soon as possible. I was getting too far behind in my true-crime shows. They were excellent teaching tools, no matter what my naysaying friends said.

On our way back to the jeep, I tried to recall any show that might help us find the truck. We had no plaster of tire tracks, no license-plate number. Unless we ran across the truck out of sheer determination and luck, we had nothing.

Back at Jacobs' farm, Harvey listened with a stoic expression as Ann opened his son's wallet and showed the photo identification. "Is this your son, sir?"

His eyes reddened. "Yes. Where is he?"

"Presumed dead, Mr. Jacobs." She closed the wallet. "We cannot tell you any more than that at this time, but do you have any idea at all where you son had gone?"

"Sure. He went hunting like most of the other hillbillies on this mountain. Sent me a text and said he got himself an eight pointer. Was right proud." He sniffed and squared his shoulders. "Some hunter shoot him?"

"We can't say." Ann's eyes softened despite her cop face. "The local authorities will be in touch with you. I'm sorry for your loss."

We turned to leave. I cast one more glance behind us before we got into the jeep.

Mr. Jacobs had retrieved a rifle from somewhere and now strode toward his truck.

Chapter Nineteen

"This is not good." I tossed Caper into the back of the jeep and jumped into the passenger seat.

As soon as we were in the vehicle, Jacobs' truck barreled past us. Eric stomped on the accelerator and sent us flying after him. "Keep trying to get ahold of Davis. This is a job for law enforcement, not us."

"Maybe not, but it's the most excitement we've had today, outside of CJ falling on that body." Mags leaned on the back of the front seat.

"Put your seatbelt on." I slapped her arm. "You're worse than a child sometimes."

"I can't see as well back here." She settled back.

"Does anyone besides me think Mr. Jacobs lied to us back there? He obviously suspects his son's death wasn't an accident." Ann spoke up from the backseat. "He suspects someone and has gone to confront them."

"Those in the deer truck?" I glanced over my shoulder.

"If I were to hazard a guess, I'd say yes."

"Me, too." Eric whipped us around a corner. "I hate high-speed chases on mountain roads."

He wasn't the only one. I tightened my seatbelt and gripped the handle above my head.

When Mr. Jacobs raced down what could barely be called a road, Eric slowed.

I scrunched my forehead. "What are you doing? We can't let him get away."

"We're staying right here. Did anyone get ahold of Davis?"

"I sent him a text. It says it went through, but I don't have any service now," Ann said.

"Are we seriously going to wait?" I glanced from Eric to Ann.

"We're blocking the road." Eric rolled his shoulders.

"What if there's another way off this road?" I pinched the area between my eyes, doing my best to ward off a headache. Eric was right not to rush into a potentially dangerous situation, but to sit idle didn't seem much better to me. What if the deer hunters came? We'd be an easy target.

Eric reached over and took my hand. "It'll be fine. All we have to do is stay here until Davis relieves us."

"We might want to move out of the way," Mags said.

Rocketing toward us was the deer truck with Jacobs right behind them. Eric shoved the gearshift into drive and spun dirt and rocks, careening us from the entrance to the road. He stopped in the ditch until the other two vehicles passed us, then sped after them.

I screamed and ducked as Jacobs fired out the driver's window of his truck and almost met a tree face-to-face. The deer hunters shot back.

"We're not doing this." Eric hit the brakes and backed up. "I won't chance one of us getting shot by mistake."

"I won't argue with that." I couldn't help the disappointment at losing the deer hunters again. "Now what?"

"We head back down the mountain and locate Davis." Eric turned the jeep around.

We hadn't gone far before another truck, splattered with mud and carrying two people wearing ski masks, passed us. The one in the passenger seat craned their neck to stare at us.

"Turn around. They're the activists." I gripped the dashboard. "If my suspicions are correct, then Dave and Lucy are headed into trouble. We need to catch up with them and warn them."

"You're going to get me killed." Eric turned the jeep around again. "All this driving is making my arm ache."

"I'm sorry." I meant it, but our friends were headed toward danger. I'd never forgive myself if we didn't at least warn them.

"Look out!" I braced for impact as the deer truck careened around the corner straight for us.

The truck swerved, barely missing the jeep. Jacobs, his truck sporting bullet holes, stayed on its tail. Behind them came the two I strongly suspected to be Heavenly Acres residents.

"This is like an episode of *Laurel and Hardy*,"

Eric said, again turning us around. "Where in the world is Davis?"

My stomach started to rebel against the race up and down the mountain. Mags had long since grown silent and sat with her eyes closed and hands clasped. I thought she might be praying. Ann kept her sharp gaze focused out the window between Eric and me. I wasn't sure what she thought she could accomplish but took comfort in the fact that little escaped her notice.

"Pull up alongside the last vehicle," she said.

Eric frowned. "A bit dangerous at this speed, don't you think?"

"Pull up next to them and start honking. CJ, call them by name. If they know we're onto their identity, they might pull back and let the other wackos shoot it out."

Eric heaved a sigh and accelerated. He laid on the horn and motioned for the driver of the vehicle to roll down the window.

"Pull over, Dave," I said, trying not to cringe at how close we were to his truck. "You won't win a gunfight."

"No idea who you're talking about."

"We're trying to save your lives. Pull over."

He slowed, allowing us to move in front of him. Eric pressed the brake and pulled to the side of the road.

"Stay in the car until I've determined it's safe," Ann said, hand on the butt of the gun on her hip. "If it really is Dave and Lucy, I'll wave you over."

A few minutes later we gathered around Dave and Lucy who had removed their masks. I glared with crossed arms. "You scared us in the woods that morning and got us in trouble with Larry. Why all the secrecy?"

"Because those poachers are dangerous people," Dave said, leaning against the truck. "We don't want them coming after Lucy's kids."

"Then why get involved at all?"

"Somebody has to." Lucy's face darkened. "They're slaughtering animals for money."

"Game and Fish is on it. The two of you need to go home and stay out of it." Eric shook his head. "You aren't equipped to tackle people like them. Are you armed?"

"Yes." Dave narrowed his eyes. "You going to take my gun?"

"Not if you go home."

I liked it when my man got tough. Unless I was on the end of his bossiness, then it wasn't quite as nice.

"Fine." Dave climbed into his truck.

"We'll follow you down the mountain," Eric said, "just to make sure you actually leave this place." He slapped the hood, grinned, and returned to the jeep.

"That was actually quite smart," I said, jogging to catch up. "Do you know why cops always put their hand on the hood or roof of your car when they pull you over? That's so if they disappear, there was proof they'd been with the driver of that vehicle."

He stopped, causing me to run into his back. "You think I'm going to disappear?"

I opened and closed my mouth a few times before I managed to push the words out. "I, uh, was just stating something I saw on one of my shows."

"Don't worry." Ann grinned and clapped him on the shoulder. "CJ isn't prophetic."

"I'm not so sure. We've spent the day surrounded by gun-toting, mountain-racing fools. I could easily disappear." He climbed back into the driver's seat and followed Dave down the mountain.

Rather than head home ourselves, Eric drove to the local pizza place and texted Dave to meet us there. "I'm starving, and I've had enough driving for one day."

A weary-looking Davis joined us before the pizza arrived at our table. He pulled up a chair and let out a long, slow breath. "Tell me about this dead body and mountain chase." He reached for a slice. "I got nothing. A wasted day."

We voted for Ann to fill him in since her days as a police officer would help her state only the facts without stating personal opinion. I winced when she named the activists, knowing Davis would be paying them an unwelcome visit.

He ate and listened, not saying anything until she's finished. He dropped the crust onto his plate and wiped his mouth with a napkin. "So, we have a dead body and a father who's trying to shoot the very people we're looking for."

"That nails it," she said.

"You marked where the body is?"

"I put an orange traffic cone in a tree," Eric said. "Unless someone returned and retrieved it, it'll be there. Jacobs' truck was pretty shot up."

"Was he hit?"

Eric shrugged. "No way of knowing. At least, I

didn't see any blood."

I personally didn't expect Mr. Jacobs to get out of his present situation alive. The man seemed fueled by revenge rather than common sense, and the poachers had already killed.

"We still don't know how Robinson is involved in all this." Eric reached for a second slice.

Maybe not, but I bet Dave and Lucy had an idea. I'd be asking them as soon as we returned home.

"Want to know what I find suspicious?" Davis asked.

"What?" Ann glanced up from her food.

"The fact that CJ and Mags are silent. Usually, when we experience this miracle, it's because they've cooked up some crazy plan."

"No plan here," Mags said. "I'm simply tired after a frightening, yet exhilarating day."

All eyes turned to me. "I'm simply coming up with questions to ask Dave and Lucy. Nothing sinister or illegal, I assure you."

"Nothing is ever simple with you." Dave narrowed his eyes. "What do you think, Eric?"

"I think she's telling the truth." He touched my leg under the table with his foot. "It's hard for her to get away with anything when Ann is around."

That's the truth. We played footsie for a while, then paid the bill and headed home while Davis went in the opposite direction.

Halfway to the community, I noticed Eric's continuous glances in his rearview mirror. "What?" I turned and stared out the back window.

Bright lights filled the car. Lights from a large truck with antlers mounted on the hood. The truck drove mere feet behind us.

"They're going to run us off the road."

"Not if I can help it." Eric pressed the gas, muttering something about rednecks who refused to go away.

"I don't get it." I couldn't peel my eyes from the looming truck. "We don't have a clue who they are. Why are they so insistent on terrorizing us?" It didn't look good for Jacobs, either. The presence of this truck left me feeling like the old man hadn't made it. We might not either if we couldn't outrun it.

"Davis is sending a squad car to intercept," Ann said. "I'm going to try and shoot out their tires."

"Be careful." Eric set his jaw and kept his gaze on the road.

Ann rolled down her window and got on her knees. She took aim.

The truck slammed into the back of us.

Ann's gun went off, shooting a hole in the roof of the jeep.

"My new car." Eric growled.

"Uh, don't look now, but is that a gun sticking out the passenger window?" Mags bent over, wrapping her arms around her knees.

I squinted against the light, trying to see. "Yep. That's a gun. Ann, wanna try taking another shot before they squeeze that trigger?" I ducked as low as I could.

"No shooting." Eric whipped the steering wheel to the right, then hit the brakes.

The truck sped past us. Before they could make a turn, we rocketed in the opposite direction toward the beautiful red and blue lights of a squad car.

Chapter Twenty

"Those guys are getting on my nerves."
Davis paced the side of the road. "They're toying
with us and I don't like it one bit."

I didn't either. In fact, I wanted to hurry home to
question Dave and Lucy. They had to know who the
poachers were.

Davis muttered something under his breath,
glared down the road in the direction the other
vehicle had sped away, then climbed back into the
squad car and motioned to Milton to drive.

The other officer gave us a nod and followed
instructions.

"Good. Let's go talk to a couple of activist
lovebirds." I marched toward the jeep.

Ann kept a sharp eye out the back window until
we arrived home. Thankfully, we didn't see any
further sign of the deer truck. I put the dogs in the
house where they curled up under the coffee table

and fell asleep, most likely worn out from the day's adventures. Poor things were too tired to do more than glance at the food I put in their dishes.

Fur babies taken care of, we headed to house number three. Dave had obviously been expecting us because he opened the door before Eric could knock.

"Wow. I didn't expect everyone to come." He stepped back and let us in.

Lucy already sat on the sofa. With six of us crowded into less than three-hundred-square feet, the rest of us stood.

Ann's cop face slipped into place. "Sit next to Lucy, Dave. It's time we got a few answers from you."

With a grim nod, he complied. "We're ready."

"Who killed Robinson?" I asked.

"The poachers."

"Who are the poachers?" Eric asked.

"We aren't one hundred-percent sure, but we suspect the new owners of number four."

"Really?" I kind of suspected something was off about them. "Why?"

He shrugged. "If we could find that darn truck, we'd know for sure. We also suspect their friend, Charlie."

"The one who volunteers at the youth center." I exchanged a glance with Eric. All things we'd suspected on our own, but again, we had no proof.

"How did you know something was going down on the mountain earlier?" Ann leaned over and peered into his face. "Don't tell me instinct or luck."

He gave a wry smile. "That truck shows up anywhere CJ is. We followed them. Did you really think you'd find the truck by checking every structure on the mountain?"

"It worked, didn't it?" I glared. "We definitely found them."

"More like they found you."

"All right." Eric held up a hand to halt our bickering. "We need to work together to catch these guys. But, first…what was Robinson's involvement in all this?"

Tears welled in Lucy's eyes. "He was one of us."

"But he liked to hunt," Mags spoke up.

"Legally hunt. There's a difference." Lucy wiped her eyes on the sleeve of her sweater. "Robinson found out who the poachers were. Even stole a cooler full of meat from them."

"Why didn't they take the cooler when they killed him?" Something didn't make sense. If I'd stashed cash in hunks of meat, I'd have definitely taken the cooler. Unless— "Is there a possibility the poachers are fighting among themselves? Maybe one is out for it all?"

"Explain that thought," Ann said.

I tried to pace, but two steps in each direction didn't help me think much. "Deer were killed. Three of them from what the police department believe. Money hidden inside each—"

"What?" Dave and Lucy asked in unison.

"I probably shouldn't have said that. Anyway, money was stashed in the hunks of meat. Robinson found poachers and stole the cooler for evidence, I'm thinking." One, two, turn, two steps more. "Yet, the poachers didn't take back the cooler. Which makes me think that the ones who killed Robinson didn't know about the money." I stopped pacing and grinned at the group watching me with wide eyes. "Makes sense, right?"

"The person who knows about the money is the one who burned down Robinson's trailer," Ann added, catching on to my brain wave. "There was evidence there they didn't want found."

"Now it's gone forever," Mags said.

"I checked the backgrounds on all three suspects, and they're clean." Ann tapped her finger against her lips, then narrowed her eyes at Dave and Lucy. "What are you not telling us?"

"Charles Campbell is really Charles Jones."

"How do you know this?"

Lucy stood and pulled a folder from under the sofa cushion where she sat. "I broke into the youth-center office and pulled his file. Next to his name, in parenthesis, was the name Jones. What we haven't been able to figure out is who wrote down the name Jones and how they found out who the man is."

"How did you find out?"

"My cousin works at LRPD. He did some digging."

From the glowering expression on Ann's face, her contact at our local PD might receive a lecture. I pitied the poor man.

"That seems too easy," Mags said. "What do we do with this information?"

"We're still working on that," Dave answered.

"Rather than chase them down," I suggested, "why not lure them out?"

"Here we go." Eric rubbed his hand down his face. "Why do you always want to be bait?"

"Because it works." I grinned.

"Let's try something different this time," Ann said. "We'll do surveillance using the security cameras you have around the community. Focus one of them strictly on house number four." She glanced out the window. "Speaking of number four, they just arrived home. We'll attract suspicion if we leave as a group."

"I need to go home, anyway." Mags zipped up her coat. "Larry will wonder where I am."

"Wait until they're inside." Ann kept watch, then told her to go. "Eric, you next. People are used to seeing me with CJ, so we'll go last. We'll stroll around a bit like she's doing her job."

By the time Ann and I left, evening had settled in and night covered the community like a black velvet hood. I glanced at one of the cameras. It would work. I could change its position from my laptop. "I still don't see how we can prove anything without that truck." I shoved my hands into the pockets of my jacket.

"I agree. Finding that truck is top priority. Let's try to see where the Langleys are the next time we spot it."

"We need to find a way of following the truck instead of it always following us." But how? The truck was like a phantom appearing at will to cause havoc. An evil poltergeist out to harm us.

I thought about the reason I'd gone to see Robinson in the first place. Number ten. We have no number ten. The email hadn't come from Robinson. I'd have recognized his handwriting. "I need to talk to Dave again."

I darted back to his house and barged inside without knocking. "You sent the email about number ten to me. You never intended to send it to Robinson."

He blinked rapidly. "What?"

Okay. Wrong guess. "Sorry." Maybe Robinson had changed up his writing. I rejoined Ann outside. "Let's take the long way home."

I stopped where number ten had once stood. Nothing there except water and electricity hookups. Think, CJ. I'd found a note tacked on the community bulletin board wanting to reserve a spot we no longer had. I'd assumed the request had been meant for Robinson and was tacked on the wrong board. I'd further assumed that they'd left off a one writing 10 instead of 110. "Do you have a flashlight?"

Ann pulled a small penlight from her pocket. "What are we looking for?"

"Just keep watch." I turned on the light and shined it around the ground searching for anything out of place.

After a tornado, anything not tacked down would have blown away. I knelt next to the electrical box and flipped up the cover. Bingo. Taped to the inside was a folded piece of paper. I removed it and stuck it in my pocket. "Let's go."

We sped to my house and locked the door. Eric had retrieved Hershey, and Caper jumped around my feet as if she hadn't eaten. Since her dish stood empty, I guessed the other dog had helped himself to both suppers.

After feeding her, I made sure all the curtains were closed. "Found something." I pulled the paper from my pocket. "It's a note from Robinson."

Dear CJ,

I'm apologizin' in advance for pulling you into a dangerous situation, but if you're reading this, then I'm dead. I've been helping Dave Lincoln and Lucy Flower stop some poachers who sell venison to local restaurants.

Tell Eric to find me at my favorite camping spot. There will be evidence that needs to go to the police.

I glanced at Ann. "Sounds like he knew about the money."

"Keep reading. Maybe he tells us who killed him."

You need to keep an eye out for a red neck Ford truck with antlers mounted on the hood. License plate EIO 236. Owner is Charles Jones, according to a source at LRPD. He's in cahoots with a man and a woman, but I haven't identified them yet. From what I've gathered, Jones stashed money somewhere. I'm not sure the other two are even aware of this.

These people are dangerous. Get this note to Detective Davis and locate the pictures. You have a knack at finding things. Study the photos very carefully. There's a clue there, but I haven't had time to find them.

Poor Robinson. It hadn't been hard to find the pictures or the money. Could the clue be the letters on the freezer tape or something else?

Stay safe, Robinson

"Where are the photos?" Ann asked.

"In my freezer." I removed the ice-cream box and dumped the photos on the table. I spread them out and leaned over them, feeling like an idiot for not understanding what the note had meant when wanting to rent number ten. Sometimes, the easiest conclusion was the one right in front of me.

"Keep looking while I move the camera to face number four." Best to do it before I forgot.

I pulled my laptop from the shelf and opened the security file. I moved the camera to where the only thing in its lens was number four and its postage-stamp yard.

While Ann studied the photos, I viewed long overdue security footage. I peered closer as the deer truck pulled into the lot and drove to the Langleys. Time stamp showed one o'clock, two mornings ago.

Charles Campbell, aka Jones, got out of the truck and entered the house without knocking. If he was pulling one over on his partners, they definitely didn't know he was. Fifteen minutes later, he left their house with a white package under his arm. Venison perhaps?

I needed to make it a habit to check the cameras every evening. Not that what I was seeing meant anything, but what if it did? "I can confirm that Charles drives the deer truck."

"Anyone with him?" Ann glanced up.

"It looks like there's someone else in the truck, but it's too dark to see." Wait for it.

Charles opened the driver's door. The dome light came on illuminating the profile of Dolly Langley. Charles leaned over, gave her a kiss, and pulled the truck away from number four. "I think Mike Langley is the third man out."

Chapter Twenty-One

Having decided Mike Langley deserved to know about his cheating wife and best friend, Ann and I made plans to fill him in right after we handed Robinson's note over to Davis the next morning. Eric sent a text that he'd take Hershey on the job with him and would see me at supper.

"Is Charles married?" I glanced at Ann.

"To someone named Kathy, I discovered." She put her phone to sleep. "Although I'm not sure the woman actually exists. We do have an address if you want to drive by there before returning home."

"You bet I do." I pulled into the parking lot and parked next to the only squad car in the lot. We probably should have checked to make sure Davis was there.

Inside, the receptionist told us we'd gotten lucky and to head on back before he left for the day.

He glanced up and frowned. "I don't know

whether to be glad or worried that you came to me rather than summoning me to your house."

"We've things to do in town." I handed him a copy of Robinson's letter and explained how I'd found it.

"I'm impressed," he said after reading it. "I'll send out an APB on Jones. Having a license plate number is good, but if we never see the truck—"

"The last time it came to Heavenly Acres was at one a.m. a few days ago. Unless they're causing trouble, they come under the cover of darkness. Like rabid bats." I grinned at my description. "We'll let you know if we discover anything else."

He nodded. "Is Larry volunteering today?"

"I don't know. Why?"

"I want to know if Jones is." He stacked some papers into a neat pile. "Thank you for your help, but I've got to go now. Cake testing with Amber, then more trying to find these poachers." He stood by the door and waited for us to leave.

I'd planned on telling him about the cheating poachers, but since he didn't have the time, I'd have to let him know later. I glanced at Ann. "Ready to visit Mrs. Campbell/Jones?"

"If she exists," Ann said. "I've put the address in my phone. It isn't far from your grandmother's house."

The white ranch-style house with black shutters was two blocks from where I'd grown up. The yard was neat with trimmed evergreen bushes. Rather than park in the driveway, I pulled up to the curb. "In case we need a fast getaway," I said.

"Right." Ann shook her head and led the way up

the faux-stone walkway.

Yard ornaments of reflecting balls and gnomes peeked and sparkled from well-tended flower beds. Someone cared about curb appeal or used gardening as a stress reliever as my grandmother had.

Ann rang the doorbell, and we waited. When no one answered, she tried again.

I'd decided no one was home when the door opened. I stared down at a lovely woman in a wheelchair. "Mrs. Jones?"

"Yes?" She smiled. "Do I know you?"

"We're friends of your husband. My uncle volunteers with him at the youth center. Is he home?"

"I'm afraid not. Charlie is working today. You should find him at the diner. May I ask what this is about?"

I really wanted to tell her what a cheating, lying, no-good lawbreaker her husband was, but the kind expression in her eyes stopped me. I hated that Charles landing in jail would break this sweet woman's heart. I did some quick thinking. "A surprise party for my uncle. Thank you for your time."

"It's scary how quickly lies can slip off your tongue," Ann said when we returned to the car.

"Not really. I do want to throw him a surprise party for his birthday in a few months. I don't plan on inviting Charles, though." I grinned and turned the key in the ignition. "Feel like stopping at the diner? It might be time to let Charlie know what we know." Time to stoke some fires for this arsonist.

"You bet." Ann held up her hand for a high-five. "Let's get this case wrapped up for poor, overworked Detective Davis so he can concentrate on his upcoming wedding."

I laughed and pulled away from the curb. Ten minutes later, a hostess in a pink dress and apron led us to a booth. When she handed us the menus, I requested that the chef come out and talk to us.

"He's in a bad mood," she said, "but I'll tell him."

"Let him know that Miss Turley and Miss Lowery just came from seeing his wife, Kathy." I smiled. "He'll come out."

Sure enough, Charles stood at our table before we'd ordered our food. "What do you want now?"

"Pull up a chair, Mr. Jones." I pasted a smile in place and tilted my head. "You're going to want to hear this."

He paled and pulled up a chair. "You spoke with Kathy?"

"Wouldn't she be devastated to know you and Dolly have a thing? Does Mike know? I doubt it. Who put the money in the meat?"

His brow furrowed. "What money?" That's a tasty bit of info. Charles might not be the traitor after all. "I haven't found any money in the venison I cook up."

Ann folded her hands on the Formica tabletop. "Does Mike know you're having an affair with his wife?"

"No. It just happened."

"Maybe he does know," I said, "and he's been getting his revenge by squirreling away some of your profits."

He tucked his tongue into his cheek and thought

for a minute. "He does handle the money." Dawning shone in his eyes. He lunged to his feet. "Leave me alone." He whirled and stormed back to the kitchen.

"Where's the truck, Mr. Jones?" I called after him.

The swinging doors banged against the wall.

When the waitress arrived to take our order, we declined. I didn't trust an angry Charles to cook anything I wanted to eat. "I am hungry, though. Fast food?"

"Sure, then let's pay Mike Langley a visit. It's fun stirring things up."

"If we turn Charles and Mike against each other, one of them might snitch on the other as part of a plea."

I made a run through a drive-thru burger place and headed for Heavenly Acres. I hadn't had time to let Caper out when Mags rushed over, face red. "Why do you keep leaving without me?"

"I'm sorry, but your light was off. I didn't think you were home." I waited on the steps and ate my burger while Caper did her business. "You can go with us to talk to Mike Langley."

"About what?"

I filled her in on what we'd discovered. "Have you seen Larry today?"

She shook her head. "He said he had something he needed to do. He's been very secretive lately. I think he's investigating on his own in a silly attempt to keep us out of trouble. It's kind of cute."

I laughed. "He'll learn not to waste his time that way."

I wadded up my wrapper and put Caper back in

the house. "You ready, Ann?"

She nodded, glancing up from her laptop. "I put in the license-plate number. That truck was reported stolen six months ago."

Did Charles really think that mounting antlers would make the truck his? "From whom?"

"Kathy Jones."

"He stole the truck from his wife?"

"I don't think she knows he has it. I bet he stole it so they could collect insurance."

I'd heard of being hard up for money before but stealing from his physically-disabled wife was an all-time low. "Let's go talk to Mike."

This time Mags went with us. After warning her to let Ann take the lead, I raised my hand to knock.

Dolly answered the door. "You're a real pain."

"Sorry to hear that. Maybe you should sell and move to a place where the manager doesn't annoy you." I grinned. "Is your husband home?"

"Mike, the nosy manager is here."

He came from the bathroom, ruffling his wet hair with a towel. "What now?"

"I'm starting to think I need to paint that as my logo and hang it above my door." I stepped back, and with a dramatic bow, waved Ann forward.

"You might want to have a seat, Mr. Langley," Ann said. "You, too, Mrs. Langley. I'm afraid what I have to say might come as a shock to you."

They gave each other puzzled looks and sat.

Mags took a seat across from them and rubbed her hands together until she noticed all the taxidermized animals. Then she grimaced. "Why would anyone want this much death around them?

One or two heads maybe, but this is a bit much."

Ann gave her a look that clearly said for her to be quiet. Then she turned back to the Langleys. "Are you aware, Mr. Langley, that your wife is having an affair with Charles Jones, and Mrs. Langley, are you aware that your husband has been stashing money in the carcasses of deer?"

Way to go, Ann. Don't hold back. Lay it right out there in their laps.

A few seconds of shocked silence, then the yelling started. Both threatened to kill each other, Charles, and anyone who got in their way. Moments later, they decided to come together in a united front and turned on us.

"Why are you doing this?" Dolly planted her hands on her hips. "What business is it of yours? Why do you want to destroy our lives?"

"Who killed Robinson?" Ann kept one hand close to the gun on her hip. Her coat covered it, but I knew she didn't leave my house without her weapon.

"What are you talking about?" Mike frowned. "You keep spouting nonsense. You act as if you know a lot, when you know nothing."

They were starting to confuse me. I knew without a doubt they were the poachers. I'd seen Charlie in the very truck that tried running us off the road. I'd seen him kissing Dolly. What was I missing?

"It's no secret I found Robinson and the cooler he stole from you," I said. "Somebody put the money in the hunks of meat. Somebody killed him." I glanced from one to the other with narrowed eyes. "You've tried to run us off the road and succeeded with Eric Drake. If not you, then who?"

"Those crazy activists?" Mike threw his arms up. "Who knows? All we wanted was to get you to back off and leave us alone. We didn't mean to hurt the ranger. We wouldn't have done any shooting if that crazy old man hadn't started shooting at us first."

"Did you kill his son?" Ann asked.

"Yeah, but that was an accident. I was shooting at a deer." He gripped his hair with both hands. "What a muddled mess this has become."

"Hold up." Mags held up her hands. "You say you don't know anything about the money, you didn't kill anyone, on purpose anyway. Where is Mr. Jacobs?"

"Home, I guess. I shot out his tire to get him to stop chasing us."

A headache started between my eyes. "If you two didn't kill Robinson, and Charles didn't kill Robinson, then who did?"

"How do you know Charles didn't?" Mike's eyes hardened. "Did you ask him?"

"No, we questioned him about Dolly and the money. Is there someone else involved in all this we don't know about?"

Chapter Twenty-Two

"No." Dolly posted hands on her hips. "Will you leave now? My husband and I have some damage control to take care of, thanks to you."

"You have no one to blame but yourself, missy." Mags scrunched up her face.

"I'm afraid that won't be possible," Ann said. "You'll both be arrested for poaching. I think it best CJ and I stay right here."

"You can't prove it was us." Mike's face turned so red I wouldn't have been surprised to see him drop dead of a heart attack.

"Perhaps not." Ann pulled her cell phone from her pocket. "I did record our conversation, though, and I'm confident there's enough here for an investigation."

"Duck." I tackled Ann to the floor as Dolly swung a foldable metal chair at her head. By the time the two of us sprang to our feet, the Langleys had sprinted outside and sped away.

Ann placed a call to Davis telling him what had occurred and in which direction the two had gone. "Now to get some kind of confession from Charles."

"I'm pretty sure these two losers will warn him before that happens." Mag rubbed her knee. "I'm getting too old for the physical stuff."

"You could have stayed home," I said.

"And miss all the fun? No, thanks." She grinned. "Let's go hunt up Mr. Jones."

"We should wait until morning," Ann said. "It's dark and cold."

"He'll run." I frowned. "The diner is still open for an hour. Let's go."

"Don't you ever get tired?" Ann shook her head. "I suffer from extreme exhaustion every time I have to protect you."

"Sorry." I grinned, not apologetic at all. She didn't pay rent if she was working as my bodyguard. I'd call us even. My phone pinged, signaling a text from Eric. I read and laughed. "Eric and Hershey will not be joining us tonight. Hershey startled a skunk and they both reek." I sent him a text to let him know we were headed for the diner.

"Girl, you won't be seeing them for a few days." Mags wrinkled her nose.

We collected Caper on our way to the car. I'd left her alone too much lately. She'd be okay in the car while we confronted Charles. I'd bring her a few bites of hamburger to appease her.

We entered the diner and asked for Charles. The waitress sighed. "You sure do want to talk to him a lot. I'm starting to think y'all are up to something illegal. He ain't here, anyway. Left out the back not two minutes ago."

Like a trio of bulls we charged through the kitchen and behind the diner. There was no sign of Charles or the deer truck.

"Drat." Mags kicked at an aluminum can, sending it careening against the dumpster. "Litterbugs." She ambled over and bent down to pick up the can. "Uh, girls. I found Charles Jones."

Ann and I rushed to her side. I moved to the other side of the dumpster where an unconscious diner chef sat slumped against a low concrete-block wall. A nice-sized goose egg stuck up from his forehead.

"Call Davis and get an ambulance over here." A sharp yapping caused me to spin around.

Kathy Jones stood there, gun aimed at my puppy's head. "Come with me, ladies."

"You're not in a wheelchair." My mouth dropped open. "It's been you all along."

"I'm not stupid. I knew what my husband was up to with Dolly. I knew what he was doing for money and who he worked with. I've been pretending for years. Disability paychecks beat working. Back to the car. You'll be driving, Miss Turley, and no funny business or I'll toss this dog out the window."

"Where are we going?" Mags crossed her arms and planted her feet. "What if we decide not to go?"

"Then I'll shoot you first, then the dog."

Kathy's smile sent cold trickles down my spine. I thought I'd stared evil in the face before, but I'd never seen darkness like what I saw in her eyes. "Don't shoot. We're coming." I cut a glance to Ann.

"Reach for that gun on your hip, and you'll be sorry," Kathy said. "Set it real nice on the ground and kick it toward me."

Ann muttered something about choking the life out of Kathy but did as she was told.

Kathy picked up the gun, tucked it in the back of her waistband, and motioned for us to go ahead of her. She scowled at her husband, then followed.

I slid into the driver's seat. "Where to?"

"Up the mountain, where else?" Kathy kept Caper on her lap and the gun pointed at me. "We've spent a lot of time up there."

I pressed my lips together. The horrible woman wasn't wearing her seatbelt. If slamming on the brakes wouldn't crush Caper, I'd do it in a heartbeat and get satisfaction out of hearing her body hit the dash.

"You could have continued on as you were with none of us the wiser," I said, pulling the car onto the highway.

"I could have if you hadn't riled up everyone. This last hour has been very stressful. Mike, Dolly, Charles, all screaming and yelling. Charles accused me of faking my disability after you spoke with him. You've messed up all my plans."

"I had nothing to do with any of that," Mags said from the backseat.

"The other woman did and you just happen to be in the wrong place at the wrong time, old woman."

"Old woman?" If Ann hadn't stopped her, Mags would have lunged at Kathy.

"Try that again and I'll leave you lying in the ditch." Kathy scowled.

Caper lay still in the woman's lap, her dark eyes sparkling up at me. If only I'd trained her to attack on command. Of course, if Kathy were to actually hurt me, Caper would definitely come to my defense.

"Turn east. I'm sure you remember where Jacobs' farm is?"

"Yeah. Why?"

"He's my father. He'll help me. All I have to do is ask."

My mouth dried up. "Sorry about your brother. His death was an accident."

"How do you know that?"

"Mike Langley was shooting at a deer and shot him."

"Oh, my revenge is going to taste so sweet."

"What do you plan on doing with us?"

"I want my money and a free ride out of here. The money is at the police department. With the three of you as my hostages, I'm sure there won't be a problem."

With Ann suspiciously silent in the backseat, I needed to keep Kathy occupied so my friend could do whatever it was she was going to do. It couldn't be anything on her cell phone from this point on. We'd reached the dead zone. Our phones couldn't be traced. I drummed my fingers on the steering wheel trying to figure out my next move. I glanced in the rearview mirror to see Mags's and Ann's heads bent close. What were they doing back there? Funny how when you want time to slow down, it speeds up. We reached Jacobs' chicken farm too soon.

Kathy ordered me to drive around the back of the furthest chicken house. I rolled my eyes at the sight of the deer truck. I'd wanted to believe her father innocent of her shady dealings.

"Out of the car." Kathy shoved her door open but kept the gun trained on me as she jumped out.

If Ann was going to make a move, now would be the time. Mags tripped and fell to her knees, putting her hand on the hubcap of my tire. I sure wished they'd fill me in on what was going on.

Kathy marched us toward the house and through a back door that led into a country-style kitchen. "Dad?"

"There's my—" His eyes widened at the sight of her holding us at gunpoint. A bloodstained bandage covered the upper part of his left arm. "This is not good, Kathy."

"We'll be out of here soon." She set Caper on the floor and ordered us to sit around the table. "I've got a plan."

"Your plan fell apart." His eyes flashed. "Your brother is dead, your ruse is up, and you'll spend the rest of your life in jail. I want no part of it."

"You always did love John more than me."

"Don't be ridiculous. Just because I don't want to go to jail doesn't mean I love you any less. Let these women go. You don't want kidnapping added to your list of crimes."

I glanced at Ann and Mags. Maybe we would have an ally in Mr. Jacobs. "Now what?" I glanced from Kathy to her father. "I assume you plan on contacting the police?"

"Of course, I do. I had to get to a place with a landline. Cell service is horrible up here." She grabbed a phone from the counter and pressed buttons. "I'd like you to give a message to Detective Davis, please. Tell him if he wants to see his friends, he'll give me all the money in the evidence room. He can reach me at this number. If I see any sign of anyone but him, I will shoot all three of these women and the little dog." She hung up, giving me a satisfied smile. "See how easy that was?"

"You're nuts." I rolled my eyes and patted my leg for Caper to jump into my lap. Her warm little body gave me comfort. I glanced at Ann and mouthed, "now what?"

She shrugged and shook her head. Great. No plan.

I studied the room noting avenues of escape. The back door, a small window over the kitchen sink, and an archway that led to a narrow hall. On the other side of the hall I could see a living room, which led me to believe the front door was there. Two immediate ways out. Not a whole lot of options when a crazy woman had a gun.

"I still think you should be mad at the others instead of us," I told her. "All I did was stumble across the dead body of my—You killed Robinson."

She gave a jerk of one shoulder. "He stole my money. I would've taken it with me if you hadn't arrived. I barely got away without you seeing me."

"His body wasn't fresh."

"Of course not." She stared at me as if I'd grown another head. "I didn't have a way of transporting a cooler full of meat when I killed him. I had to go back for a four-wheeler and smaller coolers."

"Oh." I acted as if her answer didn't seem strange. "It pays to be prepared when you murder someone."

"My daughter, a murderer." Mr. Jacobs collapsed into a chair and covered his face with his one good hand. "I never thought to see the day."

"You're the one who taught us to go after what we want in life."

"Your poor mother."

"Worked herself into an early grave with these chicken houses. That's not the life for me. I'm going to Europe and live in Paris like a queen." Kathy leaned against the counter. "I have dreams, plans for a better life. Just need my money."

"I've failed." He pushed slowly to his feet and shuffled from the room.

Great. There went any hope of him helping us. I caught Mags's gaze. "Distraction?" I whispered.

"No idea," she mouthed back.

"Here goes." I jumped to my feet and dove at Kathy, knocking Caper off my lap.

Chapter Twenty-Three

My darling dog caught the hint, even if my friends didn't and sank her teeth into Kathy's ankle.

The gun went off, powdering us with plaster from the ceiling. Kathy cursed and shook her leg trying to aim the gun at my dog.

"Run!" I yelled at the others. "Grab Caper."

Ann scooped up the dog like a football, rammed into Kathy, and darted out the door behind Mags. I slammed Kathy into the counter, yanked the gun out of her hands, and pulled the trigger. Out of bullets.

She grinned and reached for the gun at her back.

I sprinted after my friends. Keeping to the shadows, we circled the chicken houses and headed for the car. All four tires had been slashed. Mr. Jacobs was as crazy as his daughter.

"The trees." Ann headed into the thick brush. "Mags placed a tracker on the hubcap of your car. Help will come."

"Hopefully not too soon." Already the cold seeped through my coat and into my bones.

"Now would be a good time for Eric to be with us, stench or not," Mags said. "He'd know a good place for us to hide."

"We'll head for the road." Ann turned left.

"Kathy will expect that," I said, taking Caper from her. "You'll help keep me warm, sweetie." I got a lick to the face. "You're such a good girl, helping me like that. Yes, you are."

"We should stop talking." Ann moved a branch aside and helped Mags over a decaying log. "Save our energy. Temp's gonna drop to freezing."

The roar of an engine sounded behind us. "She's cheating. That's a four-wheeler." Mags stomped after Ann.

Which meant Kathy would catch up to us quickly. I confirmed this by glancing back at the bright headlight piercing the darkness. Hiding became imperative. "Remember that old barn? Can we make it?"

"We can sure try. Mags, we'll have to run."

"I can't run. Doctor's orders after my surgery."

Ann bent over. "Piggyback. Come on."

I loved my friends. If the situation wasn't so dire, I'd laugh at the sight of Mags climbing clumsily onto Ann's back. We thrashed through the woods. Dried leaves crunched under feet. Briar bushes snagged my clothing. I kept a tight hold on Caper and kept running.

"Down," Ann hissed.

Over a small hill, we could make out the shape of Kathy on the four-wheeler. She stopped and shone a flashlight around the area. She must not have spotted us because she continued past us. Thank goodness she couldn't hear us fleeing over the roar of the machine.

"There are far too many times I have to run through the woods for my life when I'm with you, CJ." Mags declined another piggyback ride. "She's headed away from us. I'll walk, thank you very much. We'll hear her coming."

Soon, the familiar sound of the engine reached us again. "She's between us and the road," I said. "I'm running out of ideas."

"We need to find the road, shelter, help—all of the above." Ann trudged forward. "We can't get too far from your car, or they won't find us until morning when we'll be nothing but chunks of ice."

"If Kathy is out here, then let's head back to Jacobs' farm and lock ourselves in one of the chicken houses. I doubt she'll think to look for us in there. Besides, if her father comes out, I'd like to punch him for slashing my tires."

"He's injured," Mags pointed out. "Besides, if I had a child as demented as his, I might slash tires too, in order to keep her off me."

"You're defending him?" My mouth dropped open. "He started a gunfight yesterday with his own son-in-law. The man is hardly innocent."

"I'm just saying he isn't that dangerous with a bum arm. I'd say Charles got in a shot."

The cold must have gotten to her brain. Mags constantly encouraged me to carry a weapon of some sort.

We heard the four-wheeler's engine as we

headed back to the chicken farm but couldn't always tell which direction the sound came from.

Ann stopped at the edge of the woods. When no one confronted us, we hurried to the nearest chicken house and slipped inside.

Oh, the smell. I clamped a hand over my mouth. My eyes watered, and my throat seized. Caper whined and struggled to get free.

"This is very unpleasant, but it's warm." Mags found a spot relatively clear of chicken poop and sat down.

The clucking of hundreds of chickens would definitely hide any sound we might make. I tried to maintain shallow breathing and sat next to Mags, tightening my grip on Caper who wanted to chase the feathery birds.

We might be warm, but I didn't know how Davis would find us. I prayed he would and quickly. I didn't want to die and become chicken food. Did chickens eat people? I shooed several curious birds away and drew my legs close, squishing Caper.

Ann made a shushing sound. Over the noise of the chickens came the roar of the four-wheeler. *Please, God, don't let Kathy look for us here.*

Shouts and pounding feet sounded outside. Mags and I huddled together while Ann kept watch. Caper barked. We froze.

The outside sounds ceased.

"Did you hear that?" Kathy's voice came from outside the door.

"Hear what?" Her father asked.

"A dog. Close by, too."

"You're hearing things. Ain't no dogs around

here."

"I'm checking the chicken house."

The door opened and the three of us sprang into action. I dropped Caper and waved my arms frantically while Mags and Ann did the same. Chickens squawked and flapped their wings running straight for Kathy and the old man. Feathers and sawdust filled the air.

We barged outside in the middle of a flock of white birds and raced for the house while Ann and Mr. Jacobs fought their way free.

Inside, I slammed the door and locked it, leading my friends into the hall. I locked the front door and coughed. "That was unpleasant."

Ann laughed, one of those head-back, full-throated laughs. "Attack of the chickens. Great thinking, CJ. They didn't know what came at them."

Mags giggled and soon I joined in with nervous chuckles which turned to a full-blown laughter fest. If Kathy and her father were to come upon us now, they'd think we'd lost our minds.

Someone knocked on the door behind me. I stifled my laugh, choking on Eau de skunk that stung my nose. Eric. I shot to my feet and peered out the narrow window.

"Let me in," he whispered. "Davis and Milton are going around the back."

I yanked the door open and pulled him inside. "Oh, Eric." I pulled the neck of my jacket over my nose and mouth. Although I wanted to wrap my arms around him and lay my head on his strong chest, the odor kept me away.

Outside came shouts and gunshots, then silence.

"Stay here," Ann said, pinching her nose. "I'll see if it's clear."

"There's a lot of chickens outside," Eric said. "I mean *a lot*."

I glanced at Mags and we dissolved into giggles. When I could compose myself, I explained how we'd managed to get out of the chicken house and into the main house.

Eric's eyes widened with every word. When I reached the end, he grinned. "That's my girl. Always expect the unexpected around Clarice Josephine Turley."

"All clear," Ann called. "Kathy and her father are cuffed. Eric, do you mind walking downwind?"

"How about you take control of Kathy?" I grinned, keeping my hand over my nose. "She would probably appreciate the attention of a handsome man." Spotting Hershey sitting next to the porch, I suggested he take the dog with him.

"I showered and changed my clothes," Eric grumbled. "I can't believe how this smell lingers." He strode to Kathy, tossed me a wink, and led the woman by the arm to the squad car.

"What about the Langleys and Charles?" I asked Davis as he led Mr. Jacobs past us.

"Already at the station. We were in the process of booking them when Eric notified us you weren't home. We checked the tracker Ann told me about when she took the thankless job of watching over you and discovered where you were. Again. Larry told us where to find Jones' wife if she wasn't at home."

"How did he know she faked the disability?"

Davis shook his head. "Larry suspected

something wasn't right and staked out the house. He caught her walking around in the backyard, did some research, and found out who her father was. We put the pieces together."

"Thanks for coming." My smile widened. "It's been an interesting day. Now I'm tired and I want to go home, take a hot shower, and put a clothespin on my nose so I can snuggle with my man."

I took a deep breath and joined Eric by his brand-new jeep sporting a few dings and scratches that made it all the more beautiful to me. He'd driven it where he didn't want to in order to help me. I held my breath, pulled his face to mine, and planted a kiss on his lips.

The End

Check out A Strange Game for Caper by scanning this QR code

Dear Reader,

I hope you're enjoying the light-hearted Tiny House mysteries. If so, I hope you'll sign up for my newsletter and also head on over to Amazon to leave a review. Thank you so much!

Cynthia Hickey

Website at www.cynthiahickey.com

Multi-published and Amazon and ECPA Best-Selling author Cynthia Hickey has sold close to a million copies of her works since 2013. She has taught a Continuing Education class at the 2015 American Christian Fiction Writers conference, several small ACFW chapters and RWA chapters, and small writer retreats. She and her husband run the small press, Winged Publications, which includes some of the CBA's best well-known authors. She lives in Arizona and Arkansas, becoming a snowbird, with her husband and one dog. She has ten grandchildren who keep her busy and tell everyone they know that "Nana is a writer".

Connect with me on FaceBook
Twitter
Sign up for my newsletter and receive a free short story
www.cynthiahickey.com

Follow me on Amazon
And Bookbub
Enjoy other books by Cynthia Hickey

Fantasy
Fate of the Faes
Shayna
Deema
Kasdeya

Time Travel
The Portal

Tiny House Mysteries
No Small Caper
Caper Goes Missing
Caper Finds a Clue

Wife for Hire – Private Investigators
Saving Sarah
Lesson for Lacey
Mission for Meghan
Long Way for Lainie
Aimed at Amy
Wife for Hire

A Hollywood Murder
Killer Pose, book 1
Killer Snapshot, book 2
Shoot to Kill, book 3
Kodak Kill Shot, book 4
To Snap a Killer

Shady Acres Mysteries
Beware the Orchids, book 1
Path to Nowhere
Poison Foliage
Poinsettia Madness

Deadly Greenhouse Gases
Vine Entrapment

CLEAN BUT GRITTY

Highland Springs

Murder Live
Say Bye to Mommy
To Breathe Again

Colors of Evil Series

Shades of Crimson
Coral Shadows

The Pretty Must Die Series

Ripped in Red, book 1
Pierced in Pink, book 2
Wounded in White, book 3
Worthy, The Complete Story

Lisa Paxton Mystery Series

Eenie Meenie Miny Mo
Jack Be Nimble
Hickory Dickory Dock

One Hour (A short story thriller)

INSPIRATIONAL
(scroll down to see clean books without inspirational message)

Whisper Sweet Nothings (a short romance)

Nosy Neighbor Series
Anything For A Mystery, Book 1
A Killer Plot, Book 2
Skin Care Can Be Murder, Book 3
Death By Baking, Book 4
Jogging Is Bad For Your Health, Book 5
Poison Bubbles, Book 6
A Good Party Can Kill You, Book 7 (Final)
Nosy Neighbor collection

Christmas with Stormi Nelson

The Summer Meadows Series
Fudge-Laced Felonies, Book 1
Candy-Coated Secrets, Book 2
Chocolate-Covered Crime, Book 3
Maui Macadamia Madness, Book 4
All four novels in one collection

The River Valley Mystery Series
Deadly Neighbors, Book 1
Advance Notice, Book 2

The Librarian's Last Chapter, Book 3
All three novels in one collection

Historical cozy
Hazel's Quest

Historical Romances
Runaway Sue
Taming the Sheriff
Sweet Apple Blossom
A Doctor's Agreement
A Lady Maid's Honor
A Touch of Sugar
Love Over Par
Heart of the Emerald

Finding Love the Harvey Girl Way
Cooking With Love
Guiding With Love
Serving With Love
Warring With Love
All 4 in 1

A Wild Horse Pass Novel
They Call Her Mrs. Sheriff, book 1 (A Western Romance)

Finding Love in Disaster
The Rancher's Dilemma

The Teacher's Rescue
The Soldier's Redemption

Woman of courage Series

A Love For Delicious
Ruth's Redemption
Charity's Gold Rush
Mountain Redemption
Woman of Courage series (all four books)

Short Story Westerns
Desert Rose
Desert Lilly
Desert Belle
Desert Daisy
Flowers of the Desert 4 in 1

Romantic Suspense

Overcoming Evil series
Mistaken Assassin
Captured Innocence
Mountain of Fear
Exposure at Sea
A Secret to Die for
Collision Course
Romantic Suspense of 5 books in 1

The Game

Suspicious Minds
After the Storm
Local Betrayal

Contemporary

Romance in Paradise
Maui Magic
Sunset Kisses
Deep Sea Love
3 in 1

Finding a Way Home
Service of Love
Hillbilly Cinderella
Unraveling Love
I'd Rather Kiss My Horse

Christmas
Dear Jillian
Romancing the Fabulous Cooper Brothers
Handcarved Christmas
The Payback Bride
Curtain Calls and Christmas Wishes
Christmas Gold
A Christmas Stamp
Snowflake Kisses
Merry's Secret Santa
A Christmas Deception

The Red Hat's Club (Contemporary novellas)

Finally
Suddenly
Surprisingly
The Red Hat's Club 3 – in 1

Short Story

One Hour (A short story thriller)
Whisper Sweet Nothings (a Valentine short romance)